I0740800

Laura E. H. Richards

Hildegarde's Holiday

A sequel to Queen Hildegarde

Laura E. H. Richards

Hildegarde's Holiday
A sequel to Queen Hildegarde

ISBN/EAN: 9783337128906

Printed in Europe, USA, Canada, Australia, Japan

Cover: Foto ©Andreas Hilbeck / pixelio.de

More available books at **www.hansebooks.com**

HILDEGARDE'S HOLIDAY

A SEQUEL TO QUEEN HILDEGARDE

BY

LAURA E. RICHARDS

ILLUSTRATED

BOSTON
ESTES AND LAURIAT
PUBLISHERS

CONTENTS.

LIST OF ILLUSTRATIONS.

HILDEGARDE'S HOLIDAY.

———◆———

CHAPTER I.

INTRODUCTORY.

IN a small waiting-room at Blank Hospital a girl was walking up and down, with quick, impatient steps. Every few minutes she stopped to listen; then, hearing no sound, she resumed her walk, with hands clasped and lips set firmly together. She was evidently in a state of high nervous excitement, for the pupils of her eyes were so dilated that they flashed black as night instead of gray; and a bright red spot burned in either cheek. In the corner, in an attitude of anxious dejection, sat a small dog. He had tried following his mistress at first, when she began her walk, and finding that the promenade took them nowhere and was very monotonous, had tried to vary the monotony by worrying her heels in a playful manner; whereupon he had been severely . reprimanded, and sent into the corner, from which he dared not emerge. He was trying, with his usual lack of success, to fathom the motives which prompted human beings to such strange and undoglike actions, when suddenly a door opened, and a lady and gentleman came in. The girl sprang forward. "Mamma!" she cried. "Doctor!"

"It is all right, my dear," said the doctor, quickly; while the lady, whose name was Mrs. Grahame, took the girl in her arms quietly, and kissed her. "It is all right; everything has gone perfectly, and in a few days your lovely friend will be better than she has ever been since she was a baby."

Hildegarde Grahame sat down, and leaning her head on her mother's shoulder, burst into tears.

"Exactly!" said the good doctor. "The best thing you could do, my child! Do you want to hear the rest now, or shall I leave it for your mother to tell?"

"Let her hear it all from you, Doctor," said Mrs. Grahame. "It will do her more good than anything else."

Hildegarde looked up and nodded, and smiled through her tears.

"Well," said the cheerful physician, "Miss Angel (her own name is an impossibility, and does not belong to her) has really borne the operation wonderfully. Marvellously!" he repeated. "The constitution, you see, was originally good. There was a foundation to work upon; that means everything, in a case like this. Now all that she requires is to be built up,—built up! Beef tea, chicken broth, wine jelly, and as soon as practicable, fresh air and exercise, — there is your programme, Miss Hildegarde; I think I can depend upon you to carry it out."

The girl stretched out her hand, which he grasped warmly. "Dear, good doctor!" she said; whereupon the physician growled, and went and looked out of the window.

"And how soon will she be able to walk?" asked the happy Hildegarde, drying her eyes and smiling through the joyful tears. "And when may I see her, Doctor? and how does she look, Mamma darling?"

"*Place aux dames!*" said the Doctor. "You may answer first, Mrs. Grahame, though your question came last."

"Dear, she looks like a white rose!" replied Mrs. Grahame. "She is sleeping quietly, with no trace of pain on her sweet face. Her breathing is as regular as a baby's; all the nurses are coming on tiptoe to look at her, and they all say, ' Bless her!' when they move away."

" My turn now," said Dr. Flower. " You may see her, Miss Hildegarde, the day after to-morrow, if all goes well, as I am tolerably sure it will; and she will be able to walk — well, say in a month."

" Oh! a month!" cried Hildegarde, dolefully. " Do you mean that she cannot walk at all till then, Doctor?"

" Why, Hilda!" said Mrs. Grahame, in gentle protest. " Pink has not walked for fourteen years, remember; surely a month is a very short time for her to learn in."

" I suppose so," said the girl, still looking disappointed, however.

" Oh, she will *begin* before that!" said Dr. Flower. " She will begin in ten days, perhaps. Little by little, you know, — a step at a time. In a fortnight she may go out to drive; in fact, carriage exercise will be a very good thing for her. An easy carriage, a gentle horse, a careful driver — "

" Oh, you best of doctors ! " cried Hildegarde, her face glowing again with delight. " Mamma, is not that exactly what we want ? I do believe we can do it, after all. You see, Doctor — Oh, tell him, Mammy dear ! You will tell him so much better."

" Hildegarde has had a very delightful plan for this summer, Doctor," said Mrs. Graham, " ever since you gave us the happy hope that this operation, after the year of treatment, would restore our dear Rose to complete health. A kinswoman of mine, a very lovely old lady, who lives in Maine, spent a part of last winter with us, and became much interested in Rose, — or Pink, as we used to call her."

" But we *don't* call her so now, Mammy ! " cried Hildegarde, impetuously. " Rose is exactly as much her own name, and she likes it much better; and even Bubble says it is prettier. But I *didn't* mean to interrupt, Mammy dear. Go on, please!"

"So," continued Mrs. Grahame, smiling, "Cousin Wealthy invited the two girls to make her a long visit this summer, as soon as Rose should be able to travel. I am sure it would be a good thing for the child, if you think the journey would not be too much for her; for it is a lovely place where Cousin Wealthy lives, and she would have the best of care."

"Capital!" cried Dr. Flower; "the very thing! She *shall* be able to travel, my dear madam. We will pack her in cotton wool if necessary; but it will not be necessary. It is now — let me see — May 10th; yes, quite so! By the 15th of June you may start on your travels, Miss Hildegarde. There is a railway near your cousin's home, Mrs Grahame?"

"Oh, yes!" cried Hilda. "It goes quite near, does n't it, Mamma?"

"Within two or three miles," said Mrs. Grahame; "and the carriage road is very good."

"That is settled, then!" said Dr. Flower, rising; "and a very good thing too. And now I must go at once and tell the good news to that bright lad, Miss Rose's brother. He is at school, I think you said?"

"Yes," replied Hildegarde. "He said he would rather not know the exact day, since he could not be allowed to help. Good Bubble! he has been so patient and brave, though I know he has thought of nothing else day and night. Thank you, Doctor, for being so kind as to let him know. Good-by!"

But when Dr. Flower went out into the hall, he saw standing opposite the door a boy, neatly dressed and very pale, with burning eyes, which met his in an agony of inquiry.

"She is all right," said the physician, quickly. "She is doing extremely well, and will soon be able to walk like other people. How upon earth did you know?" he added, in some vexation, seeing that thè sudden relief from terrible anxiety was almost more than the lad could bear. "What idiot told you?"

Bubble Chirk gave one great sob; but the next moment he controlled himself. "Nobody told me," he said; "I knew. I can't tell you how, sir, but — I knew!"

CHAPTER II.

MISS WEALTHY.

IT was the 17th of June, and Miss Wealthy Bond was expecting her young visitors. Twice she had gone over the house, with Martha trotting at her heels, to see that everything was in order, and now she was making a third tour of inspection; not because she expected to find anything wrong, but because it was a pleasure to see that everything was right.

Miss Wealthy Bond was a very pretty old lady, and was very well aware of the fact, having been told so during seventy years. "The Lord made me pleasant to look at," she was wont to say, "and it is a great privilege, my dear; but it is also a responsibility." She had lovely, rippling silver hair, and soft blue eyes, and a complexion like a girl's. She had put on to-day, for the first time, her summer costume, — a skirt and jacket of striped white dimity, open a little at the neck, with a kerchief of soft white net inside. This kerchief was fastened with quite the prettiest brooch that ever was, — a pansy, made of five deep, clear amethysts, set in a narrow rim of chased gold. Miss Wealthy always wore this brooch; for in winter it harmonized as well with her gown of lilac cashmere as it did in summer with the white dimity. At her elbow stood Martha; it was her place in life. She seldom had to be called; but was always there when Miss Wealthy wanted anything, standing a step back, but close beside her beloved mistress. Martha carried her aureole in her pocket, or somewhere else out of sight; but she was a saint all the same.

Her gray hair was smooth, and she wore spectacles with silver rims, and a gray print gown, with the sleeves invariably rolled up to the elbows, except on Sundays, when she put on her black cashmere, and spent the afternoon in uneasy state.

"I think the room looks very pretty, Martha," said Miss Wealthy, for the tenth time.

"It does, Mam," replied Martha, as heartily as if she had not heard the remark before. "Proper nice it looks, I'm sure."

"You mended that little place in the curtain, did you, Martha?"

"I did, Mam. I don't think as you could find it now, unless you looked very close."

"And you put lavender and orange-flower water in the bottles? Very well; then that's all, I think."

Miss Wealthy gave one more contented look round the pretty room, with its gay rose-flowering chintz, its cool straw matting, and comfortable cushioned window-seats, and then drew the blinds exactly half-way down, and left the room, Martha carefully closing the door.

In the cool, shady drawing-room all was in perfect order too. There were flowers in the tall Indian vases on the mantelpiece, a great bowl of roses on the mosaic centre-table, and, as usual, a bunch of pansies on the little round table by the armchair in which Miss Wealthy always sat. She established herself there now, and took up her knitting with a little sigh of contentment.

"And everything is right for supper, Martha?" she asked.

"Yes, Mam," said Martha. "A little chicken-pie, Mam, and French potatoes, and honey. I should be making the biscuit now, Mam, if you did n't need me."

"Oh no, Martha," said the old lady, "I

don't need anything.   We shall hear the wheels when they come."

She looked out of the window, across the pleasant lawn, at the blue river, and seemed for a moment as if she were going to ask Martha whether that were all right.   But she said nothing, and the saint in gray print trotted away to her kitchen.

" Dear Martha!" said Miss Wealthy, settling herself comfortably among her cushions. "It is a great privilege to have Martha.   I do hope these dear girls will not put her out. She grows a little set in her ways as she grows older, my good Martha.   I don't think that blind is *quite* half-way down.   It makes the whole room look askew, does n't it?"

She rose, and pulled the blind straight, patted a tidy on the back of a chair, and settled herself among her cushions again, with another critical glance at the river.   A pause ensued, during which the old lady's needles clicked steadily; then, at last, the sound of wheels was heard, and putting her work down in exactly the same spot from which she had taken it up, Miss Wealthy went out on the piazza to welcome her young guests.

Hildegarde sprang lightly from the carriage, and gave her hand to her companion to help her out.

"Dear Cousin Wealthy," she cried, "here we are, safe and sound. I am coming to kiss you in one moment. Carefully, Rose dear! Lean on me, so! *there* you are! now take my arm. Slowly, slowly! See, Cousin Wealthy! see how well she walks! Is n't it delightful?"

"It is, indeed!" said the old lady, heartily, kissing first the glowing cheek and then the pale one, as the girls came up to her. "And how do you do, my dears? I am very glad indeed to see you. Rose, you look so much better, I should hardly have known you; and you, Hilda, look like June itself. I must call Martha—" But Martha was there, at her elbow. "Oh, Martha! here are the young ladies."

Hildegarde shook hands warmly with Martha, and Rose gave one of her shy, sweet smiles.

"This is Miss Hildegarde," said the old lady; "and this is Miss Rose. Perhaps you will take them up to their rooms now, Martha, and Jeremiah can take the trunks up. We will have supper, my dears, as soon as you are ready; for I am sure you must be hungry."

"Yes, we are as hungry as hunters, Cousin Wealthy!" cried Hildegarde. "We shall frighten you with our appetites, I fear. This way, Martha? Yes, in one minute. Rose dear, I will put my arm round you, and you can take hold of the stair-rail. Slowly now!"

They ascended the stairs slowly, and Hildegarde did not loose her hold of her friend until she had seated her in a comfortable easy-chair in the pretty chintz bedroom.

"There, dear!" she said anxiously, stooping to unfasten her cloak. "Are you very dreadfully tired?"

"Oh no!" replied Rose, cheerfully; "not at all *dreadfully* tired, only comfortably. I ache a little, of course, but— Oh, what a pleasant room! And this chair is comfort itself."

"The window-seat for me!" cried Hildegarde, tossing her hat on the bed, and then leaning out of the window with both arms on the sill. "Rose, don't move! I forbid you to stir hand or foot. I will tell you while you are resting. There is a river, — a great, wide, beautiful river, just across the lawn."

"Well, dear," said quiet Rose, smiling,

"you knew there was a river; your mother told us so."

"Yes, Goose, I did know it," cried Hildegarde; "but I had not seen it, and did n't know what it was like. It is all blue, with sparkles all over it, and little brown flurries where the wind strikes it. There are willows all along the edge — "

"To hang our harps on?" inquired Rose.

"Precisely!" replied Hildegarde. "And I think — Rose, I *do* see a boat-house! My dear, this is bliss! We will bathe every morning. You have never seen me dive, Rose."

"I have not," said Rose; "and it would be a pity to do it out of the window, dear, because in the first place I should only see your heels as you went out, and in the second — "

"Peace, paltry soul!" cried Hilda. "Here comes a scow, loaded with wood. The wood has been wet, and is all yellow and gleaming. 'Scow,' — what an absurd word! 'Barge' is prettier."

"It sounds so like Shalott," said Rose; " I must come and look too.

> "'By the margin, willow-veiled,
>   Slide the heavy barges, trailed
>   By slow horses.'"

"Yes, it is just like it!" cried Hildegarde. "It is really a redeeming feature in you, Rose, that you are so apt in your quotations. Say the part about the river; that is exactly like what I am looking at."

"Do you say it!" said Rose, coming softly forward, and taking her seat beside her friend. "I like best to hear you."

And Hildegarde repeated in a low tone, —

> "Willows whiten, aspens quiver,
>   Little breezes dusk and shiver
>   Through the wave that runs forever
>   By the island in the river
>   Flowing down to Camelot."

The two girls squeezed each other's hand
a little, and looked at the shining river, and
straightway forgot that there was anything
else to be done, till a sharp little tinkle roused
them from their dream.

"Oh!" cried Hildegarde. "Rose, how
could you let me go a-woolgathering? Just
look at my hair!"

"And my hands!" said Rose, in dismay.
"And we said we were as hungry as hunters, and would be down in a minute. What
will Miss Bond say?"

"Well, it is all the river's fault," said Hil-
degarde, splashing vigorously in the basin.
"It should n't be so lovely! Here, dear,
here is fresh water for you. Now the brush!
Let me just wobble your hair up for you, so.
There! now you are my pinkest Rose, and
I am all right too; so down we go."

Miss Wealthy had been seriously disturbed
when the girls did not appear promptly at

sound of the tea-bell. She took her seat at the tea-table and looked it over carefully. "Punctuality is so important," she said, half to herself and half to Martha, who had just set down the teapot,—"That mat is not *quite* straight, is it, Martha? — especially in young people. I know it makes you nervous, Martha,"—Martha did not look in the least nervous,—"but it will probably not happen again. If the butter were a *little* farther this way! Thank you, Martha. Oh, here you are, my dears! Sit down, pray! You must be very hungry after— But probably you felt the need of resting a little, and to-morrow you will be quite fresh."

"No, it was n't that, Cousin Wealthy," said Hildegarde, frankly. "I am ashamed to say that we were looking out of the window, and the river was so lovely that we forgot all about supper. Please forgive us this once, for really we are pretty punctual generally.

It is part of Papa's military code, you know."

"True, my dear, true!" said Miss Wealthy, brightening up at once. "Your father is very wise. Regular habits are a great privilege, really. Will you have tea, Hilda dear, or milk?"

"Oh, milk, please!" said Hilda. "I am not to take tea till I am twenty-one, Cousin Wealthy, nor coffee either."

"And a very good plan," said Miss Wealthy, approvingly. "Milk is the natural beverage —will you cut that pie, dear, and help Rose and yourself?— for the young. When one is older, however, a cup of tea is very comforting. None for me, thank you, dear. I have my little dish of milk-toast, but I thought the pie would be just right for you young people. Martha's pastry is so *very* light that a small quantity of it is not injurious."

"Rose!" said Hildegarde, in tones of hushed rapture, "it is a chicken-pie, and it is all for us. Hold your plate, favored one of the gods! A river, a boat-house, and chicken-pie! Cousin Wealthy, I am *so* glad you asked us to come!"

"Are you, dear?" said Miss Wealthy, looking up placidly from her milk-toast. "Well, so am I!"

CHAPTER III.

THE ORCHARD.

NEXT morning, when breakfast was over, Miss Wealthy made a little speech, giving the two girls the freedom of the place.

"You will find your own way about, my dears," she said. "I will only give you some general directions. The orchard is to the right, beyond the garden. There is a pleasant seat there under one of the apple-trees, where you may like to sit. Beyond that are the woods. On the other side of the house is the barnyard, and the road goes by to the village. You will find plenty of flowers all about, and I hope you will amuse yourselves."

"Oh, indeed we shall, Cousin Wealthy!" cried Hildegarde. "It is delight enough just to breathe this delicious air and look at the river."

They were sitting on the piazza, from which the lawn sloped down to a great hedge of Norway fir, just beyond which flowed the broad blue stream of the Kennebec.

"How about the river, Cousin Wealthy?" asked Hildegarde, timidly. "I thought I saw a boat-house through the trees. Could we go out to row?"

Miss Wealthy seemed a little flurried by the question. "My dear," she said, and hesitated, — "my dear, have you — do your parents allow you to go on the water? Can you swim?"

"Oh, yes," said Hildegarde, "I can swim very well, Cousin Wealthy, — at least, Papa says I can; and I can row and paddle and sail."

"Oh, not sail!" cried Miss Wealthy, with an odd little catch in her breath, — "not sail, my dear! I could not — I could not think of that for a moment. But there is a row-boat," she added, after a pause, — "a boat which Jeremiah uses. If Jeremiah thinks she is perfectly safe, you can go out, if you feel quite sure your parents would wish it."

"Oh, I am very sure," said Hildegarde; "for I asked Papa, almost the last thing before we left. Thank you, Cousin Wealthy, so much! We will be rather quiet this morning, for Rose does not feel very strong; but this afternoon perhaps we will try the boat. Is n't there something I can do for you, Cousin Wealthy? Can't I help Martha? I can do all kinds of work, — can't I, Rose? — and I love it!"

But Martha had a young girl in the kitchen, Miss Wealthy said, whom she was training to help her; and she herself had letters to write and accounts to settle. So the two girls sauntered off slowly, arm in arm; Rose leaning on her friend, whose strong young frame seemed able to support them both.

The garden was a very pleasant place, with rhubarb and sunflowers, sweet peas and mignonette, planted here and there among the rows of vegetables, just as Jeremiah's fancy suggested. Miss Wealthy's own flower-beds, trim and gay with geraniums, pansies, and heliotrope, were under the dining-room windows; but somehow the girls liked Jeremiah's garden best. Hildegarde pulled some sweet peas, and stuck the winged blossoms in Rose's fair hair, giving a fly-away look to her smooth locks. Then she began to sniff inquiringly. "Southernwood!" she said, — "I smell southernwood somewhere, Rose. Where is it?"

"Yonder," said Rose, pointing to a feathery bush not far off.

"Oh! and there is lavender too, Hilda! Do you suppose we may pick some? I do like to have a sprig of lavender in my belt."

At this moment Jeremiah appeared, wheeling a load of turf. He was "long and lank and brown as is the ribbed sea-sand," and Hildegarde mentally christened him the Ancient Mariner on the spot; but he smiled sadly and said, "*Good*-mornin'," and seemed pleased when the girls praised his garden. "Ee-yus!" he said, with placid melancholy. "I 've seen wuss places. Minglin' the blooms with the truck and herbs was my idee, as you may say, — 'livens up one, and sobers down the other. *She* laughs at me, but she don't keer, s' long as she has all she wants. Cut ye some mignonette? That 's very favoryte with me, — very favoryte."

He cut a great bunch of mignonette; and Rose, proffering her request for lavender, received a nosegay as big as she could hold in both hands.

"The roses is just comin' on," he said. "Over behind them beans they are. A sight o' roses there'll be in another week. Coreopsis is pooty, too; that's down the other side of the corn. Curus garding, folks thinks; but, there, it's my idee, and she don't keer."

Much amused, the girls thanked the melancholy prophet, and wandered away into the orchard, to find the seat that Miss Wealthy had told them of.

"Oh, what a lovely, lovely orchard!" cried Hildegarde, in delight; and indeed it was a pretty place. The apple-trees were old, and curiously gnarled and twisted, bending this way and that, as apple-trees will. The short, fine grass was like emerald; there were no flowers at all, only green and brown, with the sunlight flickering through the branches overhead. They found the seat, which was curiously wedged into the double trunk of the very patriarch of apple-trees.

"Do look at him!" cried Hildegarde. "He is like a giant with the rheumatism. Suppose we call him Blunderbore. What does twist them so, Rose? Look! there is one with a trunk almost horizontal."

"I don't know," said Rose, slowly. "Another item for the ignorance list, Hilda. It is growing appallingly long. I really *don't* know why they twist so. In the forest they grow much taller than in orchards, and go straight up. Farmer Hartley has seen one seventy feet high, he says."

"Let us call it vegetable rheumatism!" said Hildegarde. "How *is* your poor back this morning, ma'am?" She addressed an ancient tree with respectful sympathy; indeed, it did look like an aged dame bent almost double. "Have you ever tried Pond's Extract? I think I must really buy a gallon or so for you. And as long as you must bend over, you will not mind if I take a little walk along your suffering spine, and sit on your arm, will you?"

She walked up the tree, and seated herself on a branch which was crooked like a friendly arm, making a very comfortable seat. "She's a dear old lady, Rose!" she cried. "Doesn't mind a bit, but thinks it rather does her good, — like *massage*, you know. "What do you suppose her name is?"

"Dame Crump would do, wouldn't it?" replied Rose, looking critically at the venerable dame.

"Of course! and that ferocious old person brandishing three arms over yonder must be Croquemitaine, —

"' Croquemitaine ! Croquemitaine !
Ne dinerai pas 'vec toi !'

I think they are rather a savage set, — don't you, Rosy? — all except my dear Dame Crump here."

"I *know* they are," said Rose, in a low voice. "Hush! the three witches are just behind you, Hilda. Their skinny arms are outstretched to clasp you! Fly, and save yourself from the caldron!"

"Avaunt!" cried Hilda, springing lightly from Dame Crump's sheltering arm. "Ye secret, black, and midnight hags, what is 't ye do?"

"A deed without a name!" muttered Rose, in sepulchral tones.

"I think it is, indeed!" cried Hildegarde, laughing. "Poor old gouty things! they can only claw the air, like Grandfather Small-weed, and cannot take a single step to clutch me."

"Just like me, as I was a year ago," said Rose, smiling.

" Rose! how can you ? " cried Hildegarde, indignantly; " as if you had not always been a white rosebush."

" On wheels ! " said Rose. " I often think of my dear old chair, and wonder if it misses me. Hildegarde dear ! "

" My lamb ! " replied Hildegarde, sitting down by her friend and giving her a little hug.

" I wish you could know how wonderful it all is ! I wish — no, I don't wish you could be lame even for half an hour; but I wish you could just *dream* that you were lame, and then wake up and find everything right again. Having always walked, you cannot know the wonder of it. To think that I can stand up — so ! and walk — so ! actually one foot before the other, just like other people. Oh! and I used to wonder how they did it. I don't now understand how " four-leggers," as Bubble calls them, move so many things without getting mixed up."

"Dear Rose! you are happy, are n't you?" exclaimed Hildegarde, with delight.

"Happy!" echoed Rose, her sweet face glowing like her own name-flower. "But I was always happy, you know, dear. Now it is happiness, with fairyland thrown in. I am some wonderful creature, walking through miracles; a kind of — Who was the fairy-knight you were telling me about?"

"Lohengrin?" said Hildegarde. "No, you are more like Una, in the 'Faerie Queene.' In fact, I think you *are* Una."

"And then," continued Rose, "there is another thing! At least, there are a thousand other things, but one that I was thinking of specially just now, when you named the trees. That was only play to you; but, Hilda, it used to be almost quite real for me, — that sort of thing. Sitting there as I used,

day after day, year after year, mostly alone, —
for mother and Bubble were always at work,
you know, — you cannot imagine how real
all the garden-people, as I called them, were
to me.   Why, my Eglantine —   I never told
you about Eglantine, Hilda!"

"No, heartless thing! you never did," said
Hildegarde; "and you may tell me this instant.   A pretty friend you are, keeping
things from me in that way!"

"She was a fair maiden," said Rose.   "She
stood against the wall, just by my window.
She was very lovely and graceful, with long,
slender arms.   Some people called her a
sweetbrier-bush.   She was my most inti-
mate friend, and was always peeping in at
the window and calling me to come out.
When I came and sat close beside her in my
chair, she would bend over me, and tell me
all about her love-affairs, which gave her a
great deal of trouble."

"Poor thing!" said Hildegarde, sympathetically.

"She had two lovers," continued Rose, dreamily, talking half to herself. "One was Sir Scraggo de Cedar, a tall knight in rusty armor, who stood very near her, and loved her to distraction. But she cared nothing for him, and had given her heart to the South Wind, — the most fickle and tormenting lover you can imagine. Sometimes he was perfectly charming, and wooed her in the most enchanting manner, murmuring soft things in her ear, and kissing and caressing her, till I almost fell in love with him myself. Then he would leave her alone, — oh! for days and days, — till she drooped, poor thing! and was perfectly miserable. And then perhaps he would come again in a fury, and shake and beat her in the most frightful manner, tearing her hair out, and sometimes flinging her right into the arms of poor Sir Scraggo, who quivered with emotion, but never took advantage of the situation. I used to be *very* sorry for Sir Scraggo."

"What a shame!" cried Hildegarde, warmly. "Couldn't you make her care for the poor dear?"

"Oh, no!" said Rose. "She was very self-willed, that gentle Eglantine, in spite of her soft, pretty ways. There was no moving her. She turned her back as nearly as she could on Sir Scraggo, and bent farther and farther toward the south, stretching her arms out as if imploring her heartless lover to stay with her. I fastened her back to the wall once with strips of list, for she was spoiling her figure by stooping so much; but she looked so utterly miserable that I took them off again. Dear Eglantine! I wonder if she misses me."

"I think she was rather a minx, do you

know?" said Hildegarde. "I prefer Sir Scraggo myself."

"Well," replied Rose, "one respected Sir Scraggo very much indeed; but he was *not* beautiful, and all the De Cedars are pretty stiff and formal. Then you must remember he was older than Eglantine and I, — ever and ever so much older."

"That does make a difference," said Hildegarde. "Who were some other of your garden people, you funniest Rose?"

"There was Old Moneybags!" replied Rose. "How I did detest that old man! He was a hideous old thorny cactus, all covered with warts and knobs and sharp spines. Dear mother was very proud of him, and she was always hoping he would blossom, but he never did. He lived in the house in winter, but in spring Mother set him out in the flower-bed, just beside the double buttercup. So when the buttercup blossomed, with its lovely yellow balls, I played that Old Moneybags, who was an odious old miser, was counting his gold. Then, when the petals dropped, he piled his money in little heaps, and finally he buried it. He was n't very interesting, Old Moneybags, but the buttercups were lovely. Then there were Larry Larkspur and Miss Poppy. I wonder — No! I don't believe you would."

"What I like about your remarks," said Hildegarde, "is that they are so clear. What do you mean by believing I would n't? I tell you I would!"

"Well," said Rose, laughing and blushing, "it really is n't anything; only — well, I made a little rhyme about Larry Larkspur and Miss Poppy one summer. I thought of it just now; and first I wondered if it would amuse you, and then I decided it would n't."

"*You* decided, forsooth!" cried Hildegarde. "" "Who are you?" said the caterpillar.' I will hear about Larry Larkspur, if you please, without more delay."

"It really *is n't* worth hearing!" said Rose. "Still, if you want it you shall have it; so listen!

> "Larry Larkspur, Larry Larkspur,
>   Wears a cap of purple gay;
>   Trim and handy little dandy,
>   Straight and smirk he stands alway.
>
> "Larry Larkspur, Larry Larkspur,
>   Saw the Poppy blooming fair;
>   Loved her for her scarlet satin,
>   Loved her for her fringèd hair.
>
> "Sent a message by the night-wind:
>   'Wilt thou wed me, lady gay?
>   For the heart of Larry Larkspur
>   Beats and burns for thee alway.'
>
> "When the morning 'gan to brighten,
>   Eager glanced he o'er the bed.
>   Lo! the Poppy's leaves had fallen;
>   Bare and brown her ugly head.

"Some one was seen coming toward them."

"Sore amazed stood Larry Larkspur,
    And his heart with grief was big.
'Woe is me! she was so lovely,
    Who could guess she wore a wig?'"

Hildegarde was highly delighted with the verses, and clamored for more; but at this moment some one was seen coming toward them through the trees. The some one proved to be Martha, with her sleeves rolled up, beaming mildly through her spectacles. She carried a tray, on which were two glasses of creamy milk and a plate of freshly baked cookies. Such cookies! crisp and thin, with what Martha called a "pale bake" on them, and just precisely the right quantity of ginger.

"Miss Rose does n't look over and above strong," she explained, as the girls exclaimed with delight, "and 't would be a pity for her to eat alone. The cookies is fresh, and maybe they're pretty good."

"Martha," said Hildegarde, as she nibbled a cooky, "you are a saint! Where do you keep your aureole, for I am sure you have one?"

"There's a pair of 'em, Miss Hilda," replied Martha. "They build every year in the big elm by the back door, and they do sing beautiful."

CHAPTER IV.

THE DOCTORS.

"My dears," said Miss Wealthy, as they sat down to dinner, — the bell rang on the stroke of one, and the girls were both ready and waiting in the parlor, which pleased the dear old lady very much, — "my dears, when I made the little suggestions this morning as to how you should amuse yourselves, I entirely forgot to mention Dr. Abernethy. I cannot imagine how I should have forgotten it, but Martha assures me that I did. Dr. Abernethy is entirely at your service in the mornings, but I generally require him for an hour in the afternoon. I am sure Rose will be the better for his treatment; and I trust you will both find him satisfactory, though possibly he may seem to you a little slow, for he is not so young as he once was."

"Dr. — Oh, Cousin Wealthy!" exclaimed Hildegarde, in dismay. "But we are perfectly well! At least — of course, Rose is not strong yet; but she is gaining strength every day, and we have Dr. Flower's directions. Indeed, we don't need any doctor."

Cousin Wealthy smiled. She enjoyed a little joke as much as any one, and Dr. Abernethy was one of her standing jokes.

"I think, my dear," she said, "that you will be very glad to avail yourself of the Doctor's services when once you know him. Indeed, I shall make a point of your seeing him once a day, as a rule." Then, seeing that both girls were thoroughly mystified, she added: "Dr. Abernethy is a very distinguished physician. He gives no medicine, his invariable prescription being a little gentle exercise. He lives — in the stable, my dears, and he has four legs and a tail."

"Oh! oh! Cousin Wealthy, how could you frighten us so!" cried Hildegarde. "You must be kissed immediately, as a punishment." She flew around the table, and kissed the soft cheek, like a crumpled blush rose. "A horse! How delightful! Rose, we were wishing that we might drive, were n't we? And what a funny, nice name! Dr. Abernethy! He was a great English doctor, was n't he? And I was wondering if some stupid country doctor had stolen his name."

"I had rather a severe illness a few years ago," said Miss Wealthy, "and when I was recovering from it my physician advised me to try driving regularly, saying that he should resign in favor of Dr. Horse. So I bought this excellent beast, and named him Dr. Abernethy, after the famous physician, whom I had seen once in London, when I was a little girl."

"It was he who used to do such queer things, was n't it?" said Hildegarde. "Did he do anything strange when you saw him, Cousin Wealthy?"

"Nothing really strange," said Miss Wealthy, "though it seemed so to me then. He came to see my mother, who was ill, and bolted first into the room where I sat playing with my doll.

"'Who's this? who's this?' he said, in a very gruff voice. 'Little girl! Humph! Tooth-ache, little girl?'

"'No, sir,' I answered faintly, being frightened nearly out of my wits.

"'Head-ache, little girl?'

"'No, sir.'

"'Stomach-ache, little girl?'

"'Oh, no, sir!'

"'Then take that!' and he thrust a little

paper of chocolate drops into my hand, and stumped out of the room as quickly as he had come in. I thought he was an ogre at first; for I was only seven years old, and had just been reading 'Jack and the Beanstalk;' but the chocolate drops reassured me."

"What an extraordinary man!" exclaimed Rose. "And was he a very good doctor?"

"Oh, wonderful!" replied Miss Wealthy. "People came from all parts of the world to consult him, and he could not even go out in the street without being clutched by some anxious patient. They used to tell a funny story about an old woman's catching him in this way one day, when he was in a great hurry,—but he was always in a hurry,—and pouring out a long string of symptoms, so fast that the doctor could not get in a word edgewise. At last he shouted 'Stop!' so loud that all the people in the

street turned round to stare. The old lady
stopped in terror, and Dr. Abernethy bade
her shut her eyes and put her tongue out;
then, when she did so, he walked off, and
left her standing there in the middle of the
sidewalk with her tongue out. I don't know
whether it is true, though."

" Oh, I hope it is! " cried Hildegarde, laughing. " It is too funny not to be true."

" We had a very queer doctor at Glenfield
some years ago," said Rose. " He must have
been just the opposite of Dr. Abernethy. He
was very tall and very slow, and spoke with
the queerest drawl, using always the longest
words he could find. I never shall forget
his coming to our house once when Bubble had the measles. He had come a day
or two before, but I had not seen him.
This time, however, I was in the room.
He sat down by the bed, and began stroking his long chin. It was the longest chin

I ever saw, nearly as long as the rest of his face.

"'And is there any amelioration of the symptoms this morning?' he asked Mother, — 'ame-e-lioration?' (He was very fond of repeating any word that he thought sounded well.)

"Poor dear mother had n't the faintest idea what amelioration was; and she stammered and colored, and said she had n't noticed any, and did n't *think* the child had it. But luckily I was in the 'Fifth Reader' then, and had happened to have 'amelioration' in my spelling-lesson only a few days before; so I spoke up and said, 'Oh, yes, Dr. Longman, he is a great deal better, and he is really hungry to-day.'

"'Ah!' said Dr. Longman, 'craves food, does he? — cra-aves food!'

"Just then Bubble's patience gave out. He was getting better, and it made him *so* cross, poor dear! he snapped out, in his funny way, 'I 've got a bile comin' on my nose, and it hurts like fury!'

"Dr. Longman stooped forward, put on his spectacles, and looked at the boil carefully. 'Ah!' he said, 'furunculus, — furunculus! Is it — ah — is it excru-ciating?'

"I can't describe the way in which he pronounced the last word. As he said it, he dropped his head, and looked over his spectacles at Bubble in a way that was perfectly irresistible. Bubble gave a sort of howl, and disappeared under the bedclothes; and I had a fit of coughing, which made Mother very anxious. Dear mother! she never could see anything funny about Dr. Longman."

At this moment Martha entered, bringing the dessert, — a wonderful almond-pudding, such as only Martha could make. She stopped a moment, holding the door as if to prevent some one's coming in.

"Here's the Doctor wants terrible to come in, Mam!" she said. "Will I let him?"

"Yes, certainly," said Miss Wealthy, smiling. "Let the good Doctor in!"

The girls looked up in amazement, half expecting to see a horse's head appear in the doorway; but instead, a majestic black "coon" cat, with waving feathery tail and large yellow eyes, walked solemnly in, and seeing the two strangers, stopped to observe them.

"My dears, this is the other Doctor!" said Miss Wealthy, bending to caress the new-comer "Dr. Samuel Johnson, at your service. He is one of the most important members of the family. Doctor, I hope you will be very friendly to these young ladies, and not take one of your absurd dislikes to either of them. All depends upon the first impression, my dears!" she added, in an undertone, to the girls. "He is forming his opinion now, and nothing will ever alter it."

Quite a breathless pause ensued; while the magnificent cat stood motionless, turning his yellow eyes gravely from one to the other of the girls. At length Hildegarde could not endure his gaze any longer, and she said hastily but respectfully, " Yes, sir! I *have* read ' Pilgrim's Progress,' I assure you!— read it through and through, a number of times, and love it dearly."

Dr. Johnson instantly advanced, and rubbing his head against her dress, purred loudly. He then went round to Rose, who sat opposite, and made the same demonstration of good-will to her.

"Dear pussy!" said Rose, stroking him gently, and scratching him behind one ear in a very knowing manner.

Miss Wealthy drew a long breath of satisfaction. "It is all right," she said. "Martha, he is delighted with the young ladies. Dear Doctor! he shall have some almond-pudding at once. Bring me his saucer, please, Martha!"

Martha brought a blue saucer; but Miss Wealthy looked at it with surprise and disapproval.

"That is not the Doctor's saucer, Martha," she said. "Is it possible that you have forgotten? He has *always* had the odd yellow saucer ever since he was a kitten."

"I'm sorry, Mam," said Martha, gently. "Jenny broke the yellow saucer this morning, Mam, as she was washing it after the Doctor's breakfast. I'm very sorry it should have happened, Mam."

"*Broke the yellow saucer!*" cried Miss Wealthy. Her voice was as soft as ever, but Hildegarde and Rose both felt as if the Russians had entered Constantinople. There was a moment of dreadful silence, and then

Miss Wealthy tried to smile, and began to help to the almond-pudding. "Yes, I am sure you are sorry, Martha!" she said;— "Hilda, my dear, a little pudding?—and probably Jenny is sorry too. You like the sauce, dear, don't you? We think Martha's almond-pudding one of her best. I should not have minded so much if it had been any other, but this was an odd one, and seemed so appropriate, on account of Hogarth's 'Industrious Apprentice' done in brown on the inside. Is it quite sweet enough for you, my dear Rose?"

This speech was somewhat bewildering; but after a moment Rose succeeded in separating the part that belonged to her, and said that the pudding was most delicious.

"Jenny broke a cup last winter, did she not, Martha?" asked Miss Wealthy.

"A very small cup, Mam," replied Martha, deprecatingly. " That's all she has broken since she came. "She's young, you know, Mam; and she says the saucer just slipped out of her hand, and fell on the bricks."

Miss Wealthy shivered a little, as if she heard the crash of the broken china. "I cannot remember that you have broken anything, Martha," she said, "in thirty years; and you were young when you came to me. But we will not say anything more, and I dare say Jenny will be more careful in future. The pudding is very good, Martha; and that will do, thank you." Martha withdrew, and Miss Wealthy turned to the girls with a sad little smile. "Martha is very exact," she said. "A thing of this sort troubles her extremely. Very methodical, my good Martha!"

"Hildegarde," said Rose, wishing to turn the subject and cheer the spirits of their kind hostess, "what did you mean, just now, by telling Dr. Johnson that you had read 'Pilgrim's Progress'? I am much puzzled!"

Hildegarde laughed. "Oh!" she said, "he understood, but I will explain for your benefit. When I was a little girl I was not inclined to like 'Pilgrim's Progress' at first. I thought it rather dull, and liked the Fairy Book better. I said so to Papa one day; and instead of replying, he went to the bookcase, and taking down Boswell's 'Life of Johnson,' he read me a little story. I think I can say it in the very words of the book, they made so deep an impression on me: 'Dr. Johnson one day took Bishop Percy's little daughter on his knee, and asked her what she thought of "Pilgrim's Progress." The child answered that she had not read it. "No!" replied the Doctor; "then I would not give one farthing for you!" And he set her down, and took no further notice of her.' When Papa explained to me," continued Hildegarde, laughing, "what a great man Dr. Johnson was, it seemed to me very dreadful that he should think me, or another little girl like me, not worth a farthing. So I set to work with right good-will at 'Pilgrim's Progress;' and when I was once fairly *in* the story, of course I could n't put it down till I had finished it."

" Your father is a very sensible man," said Miss Wealthy, approvingly. " 'Pilgrim's Progress' is an important part of a child's education, certainly! Let me give you a little more pudding, Hilda, my dear! No! nor you, Rose? Then, if the Doctor is ready, suppose we go into the parlor."

They found the parlor very cool and pleasant, with the blinds, as usual, drawn half-way down. Miss Wealthy drew one blind half an inch lower, compared it with the others, and pushed it up an eighth of an inch.

" And what are you going to do with your-selves this afternoon, girlies?" she asked, settling herself in her armchair, and smelling of her pansies, which, as usual, stood on the little round table at her elbow.

"Rose must go and lie down at once!" said Hildegarde, decidedly. "She must lie down for two hours every day at first, Dr. Flower says, and one hour by and by, when she is a great deal stronger. And I — oh, I shall read to her a little, till she begins to be sleepy, and then I shall write to Mamma and wander about. This is such a *happy* place, Cousin Wealthy! One does not need to do anything in particular; it is enough just to be alive and well." Then she remembered her manners, and added: "But is n't there something I can do for you, Cousin Wealthy? Can't I write some notes for you, — I often write notes for Mamma, — or wind some worsted, or do something useful? I have been playing all day, you know."

Miss Wealthy looked pleased. "Thank you, my dear!" she said warmly. "I shall be very glad of your help sometimes; but to-day I really have nothing for you to do, and besides, I think the first day ought to be all play. If you can make yourself happy in this quiet place, that is all I shall ask of you to-day. I shall probably take a little nap myself, as I often do after dinner, sitting here in my chair."

Obeying Hildegarde's imperative nod, Rose left her seat by the window, half reluctantly, and moved slowly toward the door. "It seems wicked to lie down on such a day!" she murmured; "but I suppose I must."

As she spoke, she heard a faint, a very faint sigh from Miss Wealthy. Feeling instinctively that something was wrong, she turned and saw that the tidy on the back of the chair she had been sitting in had slipped down. She went back quickly, straightened

it, patted it a little, and then with an apolo-
getic glance and smile at the old lady, went
to join Hildegarde.

"A very sweet, well-mannered girl!" was
Miss Wealthy's mental comment, as her eyes
rested contentedly on the smooth rectangular
lines of the tidy. "Two of the sweetest girls,
in fact, that I have seen for a good while.
Mildred has brought up her daughter extremely' well; and when one thinks of it,
she herself has developed in a most extraordinary manner. A most notable and useful
woman, Mildred! Who would have thought
it?"

Rose slept in the inner bedroom, which
opened directly out of Hildegarde's, with a
curtained doorway between. It was a pretty
room, and very appropriate for Rose, as there
were roses on the wall-paper and on the soft
gray carpet. Here the ex-invalid, as she
began to call herself, lay down on the cool

white bed, in the pretty summer wrapper of white challis, dotted with rosebuds, which had been Mrs. Grahame's parting present. Hildegarde put a light shawl over her, and then sat down on the window-seat.

" Shall I read or sing, Rosy ? " she asked.

" Oh ! but are you quite sure you don't want to do something else, dear ? " asked Rose.

" Absolutely sure ! " said Hildegarde. " Quite positively sure ! "

" Then," said Rose, " sing that pretty lullaby that you found in the old song-book the other day. So pretty ! it is the one that Patient Grissil sings to her babies, is n't it ? "

So Hilda sang, as follows : —

> " ' Golden slumbers kiss your eyes,
> Smiles awake you when you rise.
> Sleep, pretty wantons, do not cry,
> And I will sing a lullaby.
> Rock them, rock them, lullaby.

> " 'Care is heavy, therefore sleep you;
>   You are care, and care must keep you.
>   Sleep, pretty wantons, do not cry,
>   And I will sing a lullaby.
>   Rock them, rock them, lullaby.' "

Hildegarde glanced at the bed, and saw that Rose's eyes were just closing. Still humming the last lines of the lullaby, she cast about in her mind for something else; and there came to her another song of quaint old Thomas Dekker, which she loved even more than the other. She sang softly, —

> " 'Art thou poor, yet hast thou golden slumbers ?
>   O sweet Content !
>   Art thou rich, yet is thy mind perplexèd ?
>   O Punishment !
>   Dost laugh to see how fools are vexèd
>   To add to golden numbers golden numbers ?
>   O sweet Content, O sweet, O sweet Content !

> " 'Canst drink the waters of the crispèd spring ?
>   O sweet Content !
>   Swim'st thou in wealth, yet sink'st in thine own
>   tears ?

O Punishment !
Then he that patiently Want's burden bears
No burden bears, but is a king, a king.
O sweet Content, O sweet, O sweet Content.'"

Once more Hildegarde glanced at the bed; then, rising softly and still humming the lovely refrain, she slipped out of the room; for Rose, the "sweet content" resting like sunshine on her face, was asleep.

CHAPTER V.

ON THE RIVER.

HILDEGARDE went softly downstairs, and stood in the doorway for a few minutes, looking about her. The house was very still; nothing seemed to be stirring, or even awake, except herself. She peeped into the parlor, and saw Cousin Wealthy placidly sleeping in her easy-chair. At her feet, on a round hassock, lay Dr. Johnson, also sleeping soundly. "It is the enchanted palace," said Hildegarde to herself; "only the princess has grown old in the hundred years,— but so prettily old! — and the prince would have to be a stately old gentleman to match her." She went out on the lawn; still there was no sound, save the chirping of grass-hoppers and crickets. It was still the golden prime of a perfect June day; what would be the most beautiful thing to do where all was beauty? Read, or write letters? No! that she could do when the glory had begun to fade. She walked about here and there, — "just enjoying herself," she said. She touched the white heads of the daisies; but did not pick them, because they looked so happy. She put her arms round the most beautiful elm-tree, and gave it a little hug, just to thank it for being so stately and graceful, and for bending its branches over her so lovingly. Then a butterfly came fluttering by. It was a Camberwell Beauty, and Hildegarde followed it about a little as it hovered lazily from one daisy to another.

"Last year at this time," she said, thinking aloud, "I did n't know what a Camberwell Beauty was. I did n't know any butterflies at all; and if any one had said 'Fritillary' to me, I should have thought it was something to eat." This disgraceful confession was more than the Beauty could endure, and he fluttered away indignant.

"I don't wonder!" said the girl. "But you'd better take care, my dear. I know you now, and I don't *think* Bubble has more than two of your kind in his collection. I promised to get all the butterflies and moths I could for the dear lad, and if you are *too* superior, I may begin with you."

At this moment a faint creak fell on her ear, coming from the direction of the garden. "As of a wheelbarrow!" she said. "Jeremiah! — boat! — river! — *now* I know what I was wanting to do." She ran round to the garden; and there, to be sure, was Jeremiah, wheeling off a huge load of weeds.

"Oh, Jeremiah!" said Hildegarde, eagerly, "is the — do you think the boat is safe?"

Jeremiah put down his load and looked at her with sad surprise. "The boat?" he repeated. "She's all safe! I was down to the wharf this mornin'. Nobody's had her out, 's I know of."

"Oh, I did n't mean that!" said Hildegarde, laughing. "I mean, is she safe for me to go in? Miss Bond said that I could go out on the river, if *you* said it was all right. *Do* say it's all right, Jeremiah!"

Jeremiah never smiled, but his melancholy lightened several shades. "She's right enough," he said, — "the boat. She is n't hahnsome, but she's stiddy 's a rock. *She* don't like boats, any way o' the world, but I'll take ye down and get her out for ye."

Rightly conjecturing that the last "her" referred to the boat, Hildegarde gladly followed the Ancient Mariner down the path that sloped from the garden, through a green pasture, round to the river-bank. Here she found the boat-house, whose roof she had seen from her window, and a gray wharf with moss-grown piers. The tide was high, and it took Jeremiah only a few minutes to pull the little green boat out, and set her rocking on the smooth water.

"Oh, thank you!" said Hildegarde. "I am so much obliged!"

"No need ter!" responded Jeremiah, politely. "Ye've handled a boat before, have ye?"

"Oh, yes," she said. "I don't think I shall have any trouble." And as she spoke, she stepped lightly in, and seating herself, took the oars that he handed her. "And which is the prettiest way to row, Jeremiah, — up river, or down?"

Jeremiah meditated. "Well," he said, "I don't hardly know as I can rightly tell. Some thinks one way's pooty; some thinks t' other. Both of 'em 's sightly, to my mind."

" Then I shall try both," said Hildegarde, laughing. "Good-by, Jeremiah! I will bring the boat back safe."

The oars dipped, and the boat shot off into midstream. Jeremiah looked after it a few minutes, and then turned back toward the house. " *She* knows what she's about!" he said to himself.

Near the bank the water had been a clear, shining brown, with the pebbles showing white and yellow through it; but out here in the middle of the river it was all a blaze and ripple and sparkle of blue and gold. Hildegarde rested on her oars, and sat still for a few minutes, basking in the light and warmth; but soon she found the glory too strong, and pulled over to the other side, where high steep banks threw a shadow on the water. Here the water was very deep, and the rocks showed as clear and sharp beneath it as over it. Hildegarde rowed slowly along, sometimes touching the warm stone with her hand. She looked down, and saw little minnows and dace darting about, here and there, up and down. "How pleasant to be a fish!" she thought. "There comes one up out of the water. Plop! Did you get the fly, old fellow?

> 'They wriggled their tails;
> In the sun glanced their scales.'"

Then she tried to repeat "Saint Anthony's Sermon to the Fishes," of which she was very fond.

> "Sharp-snouted pikes,
>   Who keep fighting like tikes,
>   Now swam up harmonious
>   To hear Saint Antonius.
>   No sermon beside
>   Had the pikes so edified."

Presently something waved in the shadow,— something moving, among the still reflections of the rocks. Hildegarde looked up. There, growing in a cranny of the rock above her, was a cluster of purple bells, nodding and swaying on slender thread-like stems. They were so beautiful that she could only sit still and look at them at first, with eyes of delight. But they were so friendly, and nodded in such a cheerful way, that she soon felt acquainted with them.

"You dears!" she cried; "have you been waiting there, just for me to come and see you?"

The harebells nodded, as if there were no doubt about it.

"Well, here I am!" Hildegarde continued; "and it was very nice of you to come. How do you like living on the rock there? He must be very proud of you, the old brown giant, and I dare say you enjoy the water and the lights and shadows, and would not stay in the woods if you could. If I were a flower, I should like to be one of you, I think. Good-by, dear pretties! I should like to take you home to Rose, but it would be a wickedness to pick you."

She kissed her hand to the friendly blossoms, and they nodded a pleasant good-by, as she floated slowly down stream. A little farther on, she came to a point of rock that jutted out into the river; on it a single pine stood leaning aslant, throwing a perfect double of itself on the glassy water. Hildegarde rested in the shadow. "To be in a boat and in a tree at the same moment," she thought, "is a thing that does not happen to every one. Rose will not believe me when I tell her; yet here are the branches all around me, perfect, even to the smallest twig. Query, am I a bird or a fish? Here is actually a nest in the crotch of these branches, but I fear I shall find no eggs in it." Turning the point of rock, she found on the other side a fairy cove, with a tiny

"SHE PULLED CLOSE TO THE BANK."

patch of silver sand, and banks of fern coming to the water's edge on either side. Some of the ferns dipped their fronds in the clear water, while taller ones peeped over their heads, trying to catch a glimpse of their own reflection.

Hildegarde's keen eyes roved among the green masses, seeking the different varieties, — botrychium, lady-fern, delicate hart's-tongue; behind these, great nodding ostrich-ferns, bending their stately plumes over their lowlier sisters; beyond these again a tangle of brake running up into the woods. "Why, it is a fern show!" she thought. "This must be the exhibition room for the whole forest. Visitors will please not touch the specimens!"

She pulled close to the bank. Instantly there was a rustle and a flutter among the ferns; a little brown bird flew out, and perching on the nearest tree, scolded most violently. Very carefully Hildegarde drew the ferns aside, and lo! a wonderful thing,— a round nest, neatly built of moss and tiny twigs; and in it four white eggs spotted with brown.

"It is too good to be true," thought the girl. "I am asleep, and I shall wake in a moment. I have n't done anything to deserve seeing this. Rose is good enough; I wish she were here."

But the little brown bird was by this time in a perfect frenzy of maternal alarm; and very reluctantly, with an apology to the angry matron, Hildegarde let the ferns swing back into place, and pulled the boat away from the bank. On the whole, it seemed the most beautiful thing she had ever seen; but everything was so beautiful!

The girl's heart was very full of joy and thankfulness as she rowed along. Life was so full, so wonderful, with new wonders, new beauties, opening for her every day. "Let all that hath life praise the Lord!" she murmured softly; and the very silence seemed to fill with love and praise. Then her thoughts went back to the time, a little more than a year ago, when she neither knew nor cared about any of these things; when "the country" meant to her a summer watering-place, where one went for two or three months, to wear the prettiest of light dresses, and to ride and drive and walk on the beach. Her one idea of life was the life of cities, — of *one* city, New York. A country-girl, if she ever thought of such a thing, meant simply an ignorant, coarse, common girl, who had no advantages. No advantages! and she herself, all the time, did not know one tree from another. She had been the cleverest girl in school, and she could not tell a robin's note from a vireo's; as for the wood-thrush, she had never heard of it. A

flower to her meant a hot-house rose; a bird
was a bird; a butterfly was a butterfly. All
other insects, the whole winged host that fills
the summer air with life and sound, were
included under two heads, "millers" and
"bugs."

"No, not *quite* so bad as that!" she cried
aloud, laughing, though her cheeks burned
at her own thoughts. "I *did* know bees and
wasps, and I *think* I knew a dragon-fly when
I saw him."

But for the rest, there seemed little to say
in her defence. She was just like Peter Bell,
she thought; and she repeated Wordsworth's
lines, —

> "A primrose by a river's brim
> A yellow primrose was to him,
> And it was nothing more."

Here was this little brown bird, for example. Bird and song and eggs, all together could not tell her its name. She

drew from her pocket a little brown leather note-book, and wrote in it, " Four white eggs, speckled with brown ; brown bird, small, nest of fine twigs, on river-bank ; " slipped it in her pocket again, and rowed on, feeling better.   After all, it was so *very* much better to know that one had been a goose, than not to know it!   Now that her eyes were once open, was she not learning something new every day, almost every hour?

She rowed on now with long strokes, for the bank was steep and rocky again, and there were no more fairy coves.   Soon, however, she came to an island, — a little round island in the middle of the river, thickly covered with trees.   This was a good place to turn back at, for Rose would be awake by this time and looking for her. First, however, she would row around the island, and consider it from all sides.

The farther side showed an opening in

the trees, and a pretty little dell, shaded by silver birches, — a perfect place for a picnic, thought Hildegarde. She would bring Rose here some day, if good Martha would make them another chicken-pie; perhaps Cousin Wealthy would come too. Dear Cousin Wealthy! how good and kind and pretty she was! One would not mind growing old, if one could be sure of being good and pretty, and having everybody love one.

At this moment, as Hildegarde turned her boat up river, something very astonishing happened. Not ten yards away from her, a huge body shot up out of the water, described a glittering arc, and fell again, disappearing with a splash which sent the spray flying in all directions and made the rocks echo. Hildegarde sat quite still for several minutes, petrified with amazement, and, it must be confessed, with fear. Who ever heard of such a thing as this? A fish? Why, it was as big as a young whale! Only whales did n't come up rivers, and she had never heard of their jumping out of water in this insane way. Suppose the creature should take it into his head to leap again, and should fall into the boat? At this thought our heroine began to row as fast as she could, taking long strokes, and making the boat fairly fly through the water; though, as she said to herself, it would not make any difference, if her enemy were swimming in the same direction.

Presently, however, she heard a second splash behind her, and turning, saw the huge fish just disappearing, at some distance down river. She recovered her composure, and in a few minutes was ready to laugh at her own terrors.

Homeward now, following the west bank, as she had gone down along the east. This side was pretty, too, though there were no rocks nor ferny coves. On the contrary, the water was quite shallow, and full of brown weeds, which brushed softly against the boat. Not far from the bank she saw the highway, looking white and dusty, with the afternoon sun lying on it. "No dust on my road!" she said exultingly; "and no hills!" she added, as she saw a wagon, at some distance, climbing an almost perpendicular ascent. "I wonder what these water-plants are! Rose would know, of course."

Now came the willows that she had seen from the window, — the "margin willow-veiled" that had reminded her of the Lady of Shalott. It was pleasant to row under them, letting the cool, fragrant leaves brush against her face. Here, too, were sweet-scented rushes, of which she gathered an armful for Rose, who loved them; and in this place she made the acquaintance of a magnificent blue dragon-fly, which alighted on her oar as she lifted it from the water, and showed no disposition to depart. His azure mail glittered in the sunlight; his gauzy wings, as he furled and unfurled them deliberately, were like cobwebs powdered with snow. He evidently expected to be admired, and Hildegarde could not disappoint him.

"Fair sir," she said courteously, "I doubt not that you are the Lancelot of dragon-flies. Your armor is the finest I ever saw; doubtless, it has been polished by some lily maid of a white butterfly, or she might be a peach-blossom moth, — daintiest of all winged creatures. The sight of you fills my heart with rapture, and I fain would gaze on you for hours. Natheless, fair knight, time presses, and if you *would* remove your chivalrous self from my unworthy oar, — really not a fit place for your knighthood, — I should get on faster."

Sir Lancelot deigning no attention to this very civil speech, she splashed her other oar in the water, and exclaimed, " Hi ! " sharply, whereupon the gallant knight spread his shining wings and departed in wrath.

And now the boat-house was near, and the beautiful, beautiful time was over. Hildegarde took two or three quick strokes, and then let the boat drift on toward the wharf, while she leaned idly back and trailed her hand in the clear water. It had been so perfect, so lovely, she was very loath to go on shore again. But the thought of Rose came,—sweet, patient Rose, wondering where her Hilda was; and then she rowed quickly on, and moored the boat, and clambered lightly up the wharf.

" Good-by, good boat ! " she cried. " Good-by, dear beautiful river ! I shall see you to-morrow, the day after, every

other day while I am here. I have been happy, happy, happy with you. Good-by!"
And with a final wave of her hand, Hildegarde ran lightly up the path that led to the house.

CHAPTER VI.

A MORNING DRIVE.

PUNCTUALLY at ten o'clock the next morning Dr. Abernethy stood before the door, with a neat phaeton behind him; and the girls were summoned from the piazza, where Rose was taking her French lesson.

"My dears," said Miss Wealthy, "are you ready? You said ten o'clock, and the clock has already struck."

"Oh, yes, Cousin Wealthy!" cried Hildegarde, starting up, and dropping one book on the floor and another on the chair. "We are coming immediately. Rose, *nous allons faire une promenade en voiture! Répétez cette phrase!*"

" *Nous allong* — " began Rose, meekly; but she was cut short in her repetition.

" Not *allong,* dear, *allons, ons.* Keep your mouth open, and don't let your tongue come near the roof of your mouth after the *ll. Allons !* Try once more."

" You need not wait, Jeremiah," said Miss Wealthy, in a voice that tried not to be plaintive. " I dare say the young ladies will be ready in a minute or two, and I will stand by the Doctor till they come."

Hildegarde heard, smote her breast, flew upstairs for their hats and a shawl and pillow for Rose. In three minutes they were in the carriage, but not till a kiss and a whispered apology from Hildegarde had driven the slight cloud — not of vexation, but of wondering sadness; it seemed such a strange thing, not to be ready and waiting when Dr. Abernethy came to the door — from Miss Wealthy's kind face.

"Good-by, dear Cousin Wealthy!" and "Good-by, dear Miss Bond!" cried the two happy girls; and off they drove in high spirits, while Miss Wealthy went back to the piazza and picked up the French books, wiped them carefully, and then went upstairs and put them in the little bookcase in Hildegarde's room.

"She is a very dear girl," she said, shaking her head; "a little heedless, but perhaps all girls are. Why, Mildred—oh! but Mildred was an exception. I suppose," she added, "they call me an old maid. Very likely. Not these girls,—for they are too well-mannered,—but people. An old maid!" Miss Wealthy sighed a little, and put her hand up to the pansy breastpin,—a favorite gesture of hers; and then she went into the house, to make a new set of bags for the curtain-tassels.

Meanwhile the girls were driving along,

looking about them, and enjoying themselves immensely. Jeremiah had given them directions for a drive "just about *so* long," and they knew that they were to turn three times to the left and never to the right. And first they went up a hill, from the top of which they saw "all the kingdoms of the earth," as Rose said. The river valley was behind them, and they could see the silver stream here and there, gleaming between its wooded banks. Beyond were blue hills, fading into the blue of the sky. But before them — oh! before them was the wonder. A vast circle, hill and dale and meadow, all shut in by black, solemn woods; and beyond the woods, far, far away, a range of mountains, whose tops gleamed white in the sunlight.

"There is snow on them," said Rose. "Oh, Hildegarde! they must be the White Mountains. Jeremiah told me that we could see them from here. That highest peak must be Mount Washington. Oh, to think of it!"

They sat in silence for a few moments, watching the mountains, which lay like giants at rest.

"Rose," said Hildegarde, at length, "the Great Carbuncle is there, hidden in some crevice of those mountains; and the Great Stone Face is there, and oh! so many wonderful things. Some day we will go there, you and I; sometime when you are quite, quite strong, you know. And we will see the Flume and the wonderful Notch. You remember Hawthorne's story of the "Ambitious Guest"? I think it is one of the most beautiful of all. Perhaps — who knows? — we may find the Great Carbuncle." They were silent again; but presently Dr. Abernethy, who cared nothing whatever about mountains or carbuncles, whinnied, and gave a little impatient shake.

"Of course!" said Hildegarde. "Poor dear! he was hot, was n't he? and the flies bothered him. Here is our turn to the left; a pine-tree at the corner, — yes, this must be it! Good-by, mountains! Be sure to stay there till the next time we come."

"What was that little poem about the Greek mountains that you told me the other day?" asked Rose, as they drove along, — "the one you have copied in your common-place book. You said it was a translation from some modern Greek poet, did n't you?"

"Yes," said Hildegarde; "but I don't know what poet. I found it in a book of Dr. Felton's at home."

She thought a moment, and then repeated the verses, —

> "'Why are the mountains shadowed o'er?
> Why stand they darkened grimly?
> Is it a tempest warring there,
> Or rain-storm beating on them?

> "'It is no tempest warring there,
> No rain-storm beating on them,
> But Charon sweeping over them,
> And with him the departed.'"

"Look!" she cried, a few moments after. "There is just such a cloud-shadow sweeping over that long hill on the left. Is it true, I wonder? I never see those flying shadows without thinking of 'Charon sweeping over them.' It *is* such a comfort, Rose, that we like the same things, is n't it?"

"Indeed it is!" said Rose, heartily. "But, oh! Hilda dear, stop a moment! There is some yellow clover. Why, I had no idea it grew so far north as this!"

"Yellow clover!" repeated Hildegarde, looking about her. "Who ever heard of yellow clover? I don't see any."

"No, dear," said Rose; "it does not grow in the sides of buggies, nor even on stone-walls. If you could bend your lofty gaze to the ditch by the roadside, you might possibly see it."

"Oh, there!" said Hildegarde, laughing. "Take the reins, Miss Impudence, and I will get them." She sprang lightly out, and returned with a handful of yellow blossoms.

"Are they really clover?" she asked, examining them curiously. "I had no idea there were more than two kinds, red and white."

"There are eight kinds, child of the city," said Rose, "beside melilot, which is a kind of clover-cousin. This yellow is the hop-clover. Dear me! how it does remind me of my Aunt Caroline."

"And how, let me in a spirit of love inquire, does it resemble your Aunt Caroline? Is she yellow?"

"She was, poor dear!" replied Rose. "She has been dead now — oh! a long time. She was an aunt of Mother's; and once she had the jaundice, and it seems to me she was always yellow after that. But that was not all, Hilda. There was an old handbook of botany among Father's books, and I used to read it a great deal, and puzzle over the long words. I always liked long words, even when I was a little wee girl. Well, one day I was reading, and Aunt Caroline happened to come in. She despised reading, and thought it was an utter waste of time, and that I ought to sew or knit all the time, since I could not help Mother with the housework. She was very practical herself, and a famous housekeeper. So she looked at me, and frowned, and said, 'Well, Pink, mooning away over a book as usual? Useless rubbish! yer ma'd ought to keep ye at work.' I did n't say anything; I never said much to Aunt Caroline, because I knew she did n't like me, and I suppose I was rather spoiled by every one else being *too* good to me. But I looked down at my old book, which was open at 'Trefolium: Clover.' And there I read — oh, Hilda, it is really too bad to tell! — I read: 'The teeth bristle-form' — and hers did stick out nearly straight! — 'corolla mostly withering or persistent; the claws' — and then I began to laugh, for it was *exactly* like Aunt Caroline herself; she was *so* withering, and *so* persistent! And I sat there and giggled, a great girl of thirteen, till I got perfectly hysterical. The more I laughed, the angrier she grew, of course; till at last she went out into the kitchen and slammed the door after her. But I heard her telling Mother that that gal of hers appeared to be losing such wits as she had, — not that 't was any great loss, as fur as she could see. Was n't that dreadful, Hildegarde? Of course I was wheeled over to her house the next day, and begged her pardon; but she was still withering and persistent, though she said, ' Very excusable ! ' at last."

" Why, Rose ! " said Hildegarde, laughing. " I didn't suppose you were *ever* naughty, even when you were a baby."

" Oh, indeed I was ! " answered Rose; " just as naughty as any one else, I suppose. Did I ever tell you how I came near making poor Bubble deaf? That wasn't exactly naughty, because I didn't mean to do anything bad; but it was funny. I must have been about five years old, and I used to sit in a sort of little chair-cart that Father made for me. One day Mother was washing, and she set me down beside the baby's cradle (that was Bubble, of course), and told me to watch him, and to call her if he cried. Well, for a while, Mother said, all was quiet. Then she heard Baby fret a little, and then came a queer sort of noise, she could not tell what, and after that quiet again. So she thought what a nice, helpful little girl I was getting to be; and when she came in she said, 'Well, Pinkie, you stopped the baby's fretting, did n't you?'

"'Oh, yes, Mother!' I said, as pleased as possible. 'I roared in his ear!' You may imagine how frightened Mother was; but fortunately it did him no harm."

Here the road dipped down into a gully, and Dr. Abernethy had to pick his way carefully among loose stones. Presently the stone-walls gave place to a most wonderful kind of fence, — a kind that even country-bred Rose had never seen before. When the great trees, the giants of the old forest, had been cut, and the ground cleared for farm-lands and pastures, their stumps had been pulled up by the roots; and these roots, vast, many-branched, twisted into every imaginable shape, were locked together, standing edgewise, and tossing their naked arms in every direction.

"Oh, how wonderful!" cried Hildegarde. "Look, Rose! they are like the bones of some great monster, — a gigantic cuttle-fish, perhaps. What huge trees they must have been, to have such roots as these!"

"Dear, beautiful things!" sighed Rose. "If they could only have been left! Is n't it strange to think of people not caring for trees, Hilda?"

"Yes!" said Hilda, meekly, and blushing a little. "It is strange now; but before last year, Rose, I don't believe I ever looked at a tree."

"Oh, before last year!" cried Rose, laughing. "There was n't any 'before last year.' I had never heard of Shelley before last year. I had never read a ballad, nor a 'Waverley,' nor the 'Newcomes,' nor anything. Let's not talk about the dark ages. You love trees now, I'm sure."

"That I do!" said Hildegarde. "The oak best of all, the elm next; but I love them all."

"The pine is my favorite," said Rose. "The great stately king, with his broad arms; it always seems as if an eagle should be sitting on one of them. What was that line you told me the other day? — 'The pine-tree spreads his dark-green layers of shade.' Tennyson, is n't it?"

"Yes," replied Hildegarde. "But it was 'Cranford' that made me think of it. And it is n't 'pine-tree,' after all. I looked, and found it was 'cedar.' Mr. Holbrook, you remember, — Miss Matty's old lover, — quotes it, when they are taking tea with him. Dear Miss Matty! do you think Cousin Wealthy is the least little bit like her, Rose?"

"Perhaps!" said Rose, thoughtfully. "I

think—. Oh, Hilda, look!" she cried, breaking off suddenly. "What a queer little house!"

Hildegarde checked Dr. Abernethy, who had been trotting along quite briskly, and they both looked curiously at the little house on their left, which certainly was "queer," — a low, unpainted shanty, gray with age, the shingles rotting off, and moss growing in the chinks. The small panes of glass were crusted with dirt, and here and there one had been broken, and replaced with brown paper. The front yard was a tangle of ribbon-grass and clover; but a tuft of straggling flowers here and there showed that it had once had care and attention. There was no sign of life about the place.

"Rose!" cried Hildegarde, stopping the horse with a pull of the reins; "it is a deserted house. Do you know that I have never seen one in my life? I must positively take a peep at it, and see what it is like inside. Take the reins, Bonne Silène, while I go and reconnoitre the position." She jumped out, and making her way as best she might through the grassy tangle, was soon gazing in at one of the windows. "Oh!" she cried, "it *is n't* deserted, Rose! At least — well, some one has been here. But, oh, me! oh, *me!* What a place! I never, never dreamed of such a place. I—"

"What *is* the matter?" cried Rose. "If you don't tell me, I shall jump out!"

"No, you won't!" said Hildegarde. "You'd better not, Miss! but *oh*, dear! who ever, ever dreamed of such a place? My dear, it is the Abode of Dirt. Squalid is no word for it; squalor is richness compared to this house. I am looking — sit still, Rose! — I am looking into a room about as big as a comfortable pantry. There is a broken stove in it, and a table, and a stool; and in the room beyond I can see a bed, — at least, I suppose it is meant for a bed. Oh! what person *can* live here?"

"*I am coming*, Hilda," said Rose. "The only question is whether I get out with your help or without."

"Obstinate Thing!" cried Hildegarde, flying to her assistance. "Well, it shall see the lovely sight, so it shall. Carefully, now; don't trip on these long grass-loops. There! is n't that a pretty place? Now enjoy yourself, while I get out the tie-rein, and fasten the good beast to a tree."

In hunting for the tie-rein under the seat of the carriage, Hildegarde discovered something else which made her utter an exclamation of surprise. "Luncheon!" she cried. "Rose, my dear, did you know about this basket? Saint Martha must have put it in. Turnovers, Rose! sandwiches, Rose! and, I declare, a bottle of milk and a tin cup. Were ever two girls so spoiled as we shall be?"

"How kind!" said Rose. "I am not in the least hungry, but I *should* like a cup of milk. Oh, Hildegarde!"

"What now?" asked that young woman, returning with the precious basket, and applying her nose once more to the window. "Fresh horrors?"

"My dear," said Rose, "look! That is the pantry, — that little cupboard, with the door hanging by one hinge; and there is n't anything in it to eat, except three crackers and an onion."

Both girls gazed in silence at the forlorn scene before them. Then they looked at each other. Hildegarde gave an expressive little shake to the basket. Rose smiled and nodded; then they hugged each other a little, which was a foolish way they had when they were pleased. Very cautiously Hildegarde pushed the crazy door open, and they stood in the melancholy little hovel. All was even dirtier and more squalid than it had looked from outside; but the girls did not mind it now, for they had an idea, which had come perhaps to both at the same moment. Hilda looked about for a broom, and finally found the dilapidated skeleton of one. Rose, realizing at once that search for a duster would be fruitless, pulled a double handful of long grass from the front yard, and the two laid about them, — one vigorously, the other carefully and thoroughly. Dust flew from doors and windows; the girls sneezed and coughed, but persevered, till the little room at last began to look as if it might once have been habitable.

"Now you have done enough, Rosy!" cried Hildegarde. "Sit down on the door-step and make a posy, while I finish."

Rose, being rather tired, obeyed. Hildegarde then looked for a scrubbing-brush, but finding none, was obliged to give the little black table such a cleaning as she could with the broom and bunches of grass. Behind the house was a lilac-bush, covered with lovely fragrant clusters of blossoms; she gathered a huge bunch of them, and putting them in a broken pitcher with water, set them in the middle of the table. Meanwhile Rose had found two or three peonies and some sweet-william, and with these and some ribbon-grass had made quite a brilliant bouquet, which was laid beside the one cracked plate which the cupboard afforded. On this plate the sandwiches were neatly piled, and the turnovers (all but two, which the girls ate, partly out of gratitude to Martha, but chiefly because they were good) were laid on a cluster of green leaves. As for the milk, that, Hildegarde declared, Rose must and should drink; and she stood over her till she tilted the bottle back and drained the last drop.

"Oh, dear!" said Rose, looking sadly at the empty bottle; "I hope the poor thing does n't like milk. It could n't be a child, Hildegarde, could it? living here all alone. And anyhow he — or she — will have a better dinner than one onion and — " But here she broke off, and uttered a low cry of dismay. "Oh, Hilda! Hilda! look there!"

Hildegarde turned hastily round, and then stood petrified with dismay; for some one was looking in at the window. Pressed against the little back window was the face of an old man, so withered and wrinkled that it looked hardly human; only the eyes, bright and keen, were fixed upon the girls, with what they thought was a look of anger. Masses of wild, unkempt gray hair surrounded the face, and a fragment of old straw hat was drawn down over the brows. Altogether it was a wild vision; and perhaps it was not surprising that the gentle Rose was terrified,

"SOME ONE WAS LOOKING IN AT THE WINDOW."

while even Hildegarde felt decidedly uncomfortable. They stood still for a moment, meeting helplessly the steady gaze of the sharp, fierce eyes; then with one impulse they turned and fled, — Hildegarde half carrying her companion in her strong arms. Half laughing, half crying, they reached the carriage. Rose tumbled in somehow, Hildegarde flew to unfasten the tie-rein; and the next moment they were speeding away at quite a surprising rate, Dr. Abernethy having, for the first time in years, received a smart touch of the whip, which filled him with amazement and indignation.

Neither of the girls spoke until at least a quarter of a mile lay between them and the scene of their terror; then, as they came to the foot of a hill, Hildegarde checked the good horse to a walk, and turned and looked at Rose. One look, —and they both broke into fits of laughter, and laughed and laughed as if they never would stop.

"Oh!" cried Hildegarde, wiping the tears which were rolling down her cheeks. "Rose! I wonder if I looked as guilty as I felt. No wonder he glowered, if I did."

"Of course you did," said Rose. "You were the perfect ideal of a Female Burgler, caught with the spoons in her hand; and I —oh! my cheeks are burning still; I feel as if I were nothing but a blush. And after all, we *were* breaking and entering, Hilda!"

"But we did no harm!" said Hilda, stoutly. "I don't much care, now we are safe out of the way. And I'm glad the poor old glowering thing will have a good dinner for once. Rose, he must be at least a hundred! Did you ever see anything look so old?"

Rose shook her head meditatively. "It's dreadful to think of his living all alone there," she said. "For he must be alone. There was only one plate, you know, and that wretched bed. Oh, Hilda!" she added, a moment later, "the basket! we have left the basket there. What shall we do? Must we go back?"

"Perish the thought!" cried Hildegarde, with a shudder half real, half playful. "I would n't go back there now for the half of my kingdom. Let me see! We will not tell Cousin Wealthy to-day—"

"Oh, no!" cried Rose, shrinking at the bare thought.

"Nor even to-morrow, perhaps," continued Hildegarde. "She would be frightened, and might expect you to be ill; we will wait a day or two before we tell her. But Martha is not nervous. We can tell her to-morrow, and say that we will get another basket. After all, we were doing no harm,—none in the world."

But the best-laid plans, as we all know,

" gang aft agley ; " and the girls were not
to have the telling of their adventure in their
own way.

That evening, as they were sitting on the
piazza after tea, they heard Miss Wealthy's
voice, saying, " Martha, there is some one
coming up the front walk, — an aged man,
apparently. Will you see who it is, please ?
Perhaps he wants food, for I see he has a
basket."

Hildegarde and Rose looked at each other
in terror.

" Oh, Hilda ! " whispered Rose, catching
her friend's hand, " it must be he ! What
shall we do ? "

" Hush ! " said Hildegarde. " Listen, and
don't be a goose ! Do ? what should he do to
us ? He might recite the ' Curse of Kehama,'
but it is n't likely he knows it."

Martha, who had been reconnoitring
through a crack of the window-blind, now

uttered an exclamation. "Well, of all! Mam, it's old Galusha Pennypacker, as sure as you stand there."

"Is it possible?" said Miss Wealthy, in a tone of great surprise. "Martha, you *must* be mistaken. Galusha Pennypacker coming here. Why *should* he come here?"

But for once Martha was not ready to answer her mistress, for she had gone to open the door.

The girls listened, with clasped hands and straining ears.

"Why, Mr. Pennypacker!" they heard Martha say. "This is never you?"

Then a shrill, cracked voice broke in, speaking very slowly, as if speech were an unaccustomed effort. "Is there — two gals — here?"

"Two gals?" repeated Martha, in amazement. "What two gals?"

"Gals!" said the old man's voice, — "one

on 'em highty-tighty, fly-away-lookin', 'n' the other kind o' 'pindlin'; drivin' your hoss, they was."

"Why — yes!" said Martha, more and more astonished. "What upon earth —"

"Here's their basket!" the old man continued; "tell 'em I — relished the victuals. Good-day t' ye!"

Then came the sound of a stick on ·the steps, and of shuffling feet on the gravel; and the next moment Miss Wealthy and Martha were gazing at the guilty girls with faces of mute amazement and inquiry which almost upset Hildegarde's composure.

"It's true, Cousin Wealthy!" she said quickly. "We meant to tell you — in a little while, when you would not be worried. We thought the house was deserted, and I went and looked in at the window. And — it looked so wretched, we thought we might —"

"There was only an onion and three crackers," murmured Rose, in deprecating parenthesis.

"We thought we might leave part of our luncheon, for Martha had given us such a quantity; and just when we had finished, we saw a face at the window — oh, such a dreadful old face! — and we ran away, and forgot the basket. So you see, Martha," she added, "it was partly your fault, for giving us so much luncheon."

"I see!" said Martha, chuckling, and apparently much amused.

But Miss Wealthy looked really frightened. "My *dear* girls," she said, "it was a *very* imprudent thing to do. Why, Galusha Pennypacker is half insane, people think. A dreadful old miser, who lives in filth and wretchedness, while he has plenty of money hidden away, — at least people say he has. Why, it terrifies me to think of your going into that hovel."

" Oh! Cousin Wealthy," said Hildegarde, soothingly, " he could n't have hurt us, poor old thing! if he had tried. He looks at least a hundred years old. And of course we did n't know he was a miser. But surely it will do no harm for him to have a good dinner for once, and Martha's turnovers ought really to have a civilizing effect upon him. Who knows? Perhaps it may make him remember nicer ways, and he may try to do better."

Miss Wealthy was partly reconciled by this view of the case; but she declared that Rose must go to bed at once, as she must be quite exhausted.

At this moment Martha, who was still holding the basket, gave an exclamation of surprise. " Why," she said, " there 's things in this! Did you leave these in the basket, Miss Hilda?"

" I? No!" cried Hildegarde, wondering. "I left nothing at all in it. What is there?"

All clustered eagerly round Martha, who with provoking deliberation took out two small parcels which lay in the bottom of the basket, and looked them carefully over before opening them. They were wrapped in dirty scraps of brown paper.

"Oh! there is writing on them!" cried Hildegarde. "Martha dear, *do* tell us what it says!"

Martha studied the inscriptions for some minutes, and then read aloud: "'The fly-away gal' and 'the pail gal.' Well, of all!" she cried, "it's presents, I do believe. Here, Miss Hilda, this must be for you."

Hildegarde opened the little parcel eagerly. It contained a small shagreen case, which in its turn proved to contain a pair of scissors of antique and curious form, an ivory tablet, yellow with age, a silver bodkin, and a silver fruit-knife, all fitting neatly in their places; the whole case closing with a spring. "It is the prettiest thing I ever saw!" cried Hildegarde. "See, Cousin Wealthy, is n't it delightful to think of that poor old dear— But what have you, Rose-red? You must be the 'pail gal,' of course, though you are not pale now."

Rose opened her parcel, and found, in a tiny box of faded morocco, an ivory thimble exquisitely carved with minute Chinese figures. It fitted her slender finger to perfection, and she gazed at it with great delight, while Miss Wealthy and Martha shook their heads in amazement and perplexity.

"Galusha Pennypacker, with such things as these!" cried one.

"Galusha Pennypacker making presents!" exclaimed the other. "Well, wonders will never cease!"

"The thimble is really beautiful!" said Miss Wealthy. "He was a seafaring man in his youth, I remember, and he must have brought this home from one of his voyages, perhaps fifty or sixty years ago. Dear me! how strangely things do come about! But, my dear Rose, you really *must* go to bed at once, for I am sure you must be quite exhausted."

And the delighted girls went off in triumph with their treasures, to chatter in their rooms as only girls can chatter.

CHAPTER VII.

A "STORY EVENING."

THE next evening was chilly, and instead of sitting on the piazza, the girls were glad to draw their chairs around Miss Wealthy's work-table and bring out their work-baskets. Hildegarde had brought two dozen napkins with her to hem for her mother, and Rose was knitting a soft white cloud, which was to be a Christmas present for good Mrs. Hartley at the farm. As for Miss Wealthy, she, as usual, was knitting gray stockings of fine soft wool. They all fell to talking about old Galusha Pennypacker, now pitying his misery, now wondering at the tales of his avarice. Hildegarde took out the little scissors-case, and examined it anew. "Do you suppose this belonged to his mother?" she asked. "You say he never married. Or had he a sister?"

"No, he had no sister," replied Miss Wealthy. "His mother was a very respectable woman. I remember her, though she died when I was quite a little girl. He had an aunt, too, — a singular woman, who used to be very kind to me. What is it, my dear?" For Hildegarde had given a little cry of surprise.

"Here is a name!" cried the girl. "At least, it looks like a name; but I cannot make it out. See, Cousin Wealthy, on the little tablet! Oh, how interesting!"

Miss Wealthy took the tablet, which consisted of two thin leaves of ivory, fitting closely together. On the inside of one leaf was written in pencil, in a tremulous hand, "Ca-ira."

"Is it a name?" asked Rose.

Miss Wealthy nodded. "His aunt's name," she said, — "Ca-iry[1] Pennypacker. Yes, surely; this must have belonged to her. Dear, dear! how strangely things come about! Aunt Ca-iry we all called her, though she was no connection of ours. And to think of your having her scissors-case! Now I come to remember, I used to see this in her basket when I used to poke over her things, as I loved to do. Dear, dear!"

"Oh, Cousin Wealthy," cried Hildegarde, "*do* tell us about her, please! How came she to have such a queer name? I am sure there must be some delightful story about her."

Miss Wealthy considered a minute, then she said: "My dear, if you will open the fourth left-hand drawer of that chest between

---

[1] Pronounced Kay-iry.

the windows, and look in the farther right-hand corner of the drawer, I think you will find a roll of paper tied with a pink ribbon."

Hildegarde obeyed in wondering silence; and Miss Wealthy, taking the roll, held it in her hand for a moment without speaking, which was very trying to the girls' feelings. At last she said,—

"There *is* an interesting story about Ca-iry Pennypacker, and, curiously enough, I have it here, written down by — whom do you think? — your mother, Hilda, my dear!"

"My mother!" cried Hildegarde, in amazement.

"Your mother," repeated Miss Wealthy. "You see, when Mildred was a harum-scarum girl—" Hildegarde uttered an exclamation, and Miss Wealthy stopped short. "Is there something you want to say, dear?" she asked gently. "I will wait."

The girl blushed violently. "I beg your

pardon, Cousin Wealthy," she said humbly. "Shall I go out and stand in the entry? Papa always used to make me, when I interrupted."

"You are rather too big for that now, my child," said the old lady, smiling; "and I notice that you very seldom interrupt. It is better *never* done, however. Well, as I was saying, your mother used to make me a great many visits in her school holidays; for she was my god-daughter, and always very dear to me. She was very fond of hearing stories, and I told her all the old tales I could think of, — among them this one of Aunt Ca-iry's, which the old lady had told me herself when I was perhaps ten years old. It had made a deep impression on me, so that I was able to repeat it almost in her own words, in the country talk she always used. She was not an educated woman, my dear, but one of sterling good sense and strong character. Well, the story impressed your mother so much that she was very anxious for me to write it down; but as I have no gift whatever in that way, she finally wrote it herself, taking it from my lips, as you may say, — only changing my name from Wealthy to Dolly, — but making it appear as if the old woman herself were speaking. Very apt at that sort of thing Mildred always was. And now, if you like, my dears, I will read you the story."

If they liked! Was there ever a girl who did not love a story? Gray eyes and blue sparkled with anticipation, and there was no further danger of interruption as Miss Wealthy, in her soft, clear voice, began to read the story of —

CA-IRY AND THE QUEEN.

What's this you 've found? Well, now! well, now! where did you get that, little gal? Been rummagin' in Aunt Ca-iry's bureau, hev you?

Naughty little gal! Bring it to me, honey. Why, that little bag, — I would n't part with it for gold! That was give me by a queen, — think o' that, Dolly, — by a real live queen, 'cordin' to her own idees, — the Queen o' Sheba.

Tell you about her? Why, yes, I will. Bring your little cheer here by the fire, — so; and get your knittin'. When little gals come to spend the day with Aunt Ca-iry they allus brings their knittin', — don't they? — 'cause they know they won't get any story unless they do. I can't have no idle hands round this kitchen, 'cause Satan might git in, ye know, and find some mischief for them to do. There! now we 're right comf'table, and I 'll begin.

You see, Dolly, I 've lived alone most o' my life, as you may say. Mother died when I was fifteen, and Father, he could n't stay on without her, so he went the next year; and my brother was settled a good way off: so ever since I 've lived here in the old brown house alone, 'cept for the time I 'm goin' to tell ye about, when I had a boarder, and a queer one she was. Plenty o' folks asked me to hire out with them, or board with them, and I s'pose I might have married, if I 'd been that kind, but I was n't. Never could abide the thought of havin' a man gormineerin' over me, not if he was the lord o' the land. And I was strong, and had a cow and some fowls, and altogether I knew when I was well off; and after a while folks learned to let me alone. "Queer Ca-iry," they called me, — in your grandfather's time, Dolly, — but now it's "Aunt Ca-iry" with the hull country round, and everybody's very good to the old woman.

How did I come to have such a funny name? Well, my father give it to me. He was a great man for readin', my father was, and there was one book he could n't ever let alone, skurcely. 'T was about the French Revolution, and it told how the French people tried to git up a republic like ourn. But they had n't no sense, seemin'ly, and some of 'em was no better nor wild beasts, with their slaughterin', devourin' ways; so nothin' much came of it in the end 'cept bloodshed.

Well, it seems they had a way of yellin' round the streets, and shoutin' and singin', "Ca-ira! Ca-ira!" Made a song out of it, the book said, and sang it day in and day out. Father said it meant "That will go!" or somethin' like that, though I never could see any meanin' in it myself. Anyhow, it took Father's fancy greatly, and when I was born, nothin' would do but I must be christened Ca-ira. So I was, and so I stayed; and I don't know as I should have done any better if I 'd been called Susan or Jerusha. So that 's all about the name, and now we 'll come to the story.

One day, when I was about eighteen years old, I was takin' a walk in the woods with my dog Bluff. I was very fond o' walkin', and so was Bluff, and there was woods all about, twice as much as there is now. It was a fine, clear day, and we wandered a 'long way, further from home than we often went, 'way down by Rollin' Dam Falls. The stream was full, and the falls were a pretty sight; and I sat lookin' at 'em, as girls do, and pullin' wintergreen leaves. I never smell wintergreen now without thinkin' of that day. All of a suddent I heard Bluff bark; and lookin' round, I saw him snuffin' and smellin' about a steep clay bank covered with vines and brambles. "Woodchuck!" I thought; and I called him off, for I never let him kill critters unless they were mischeevous, which in the wild woods they could n't be, of course. But the dog would n't come off. He stayed there, sniffin' and growlin', and at last I went to see what the trouble was.

My dear, when I lifted up those vines and brambles, what should I see but a hole in the bank! — a hole about two feet across, bigger than any that a woodchuck ever made. The edges were rubbed smooth, as if the critter that made it was big enough to fit pretty close in gettin' through. My first idee was that 't was a wolf's den, — wolves were seen sometimes in those days in the Cobbossee woods, — and I was goin' to drop the vines and slip off as quiet as I could, when what does that dog do but pop into the hole right before my eyes, and go wrigglin' through it! I called and whistled, but 't was no use; the dog was bound to see what was in there.

I waited a minute, expectin' to hear the wolf growl, and thinkin' my poor Bluff would be torn to pieces, and yet I must go off and leave him, or be treated the same myself. But, Dolly, instead of a wolf's growl, I heard next minute a sound that made me start more 'n the wolf would ha' done, — the sound of a human voice. Yes! out o' the bowels o' the earth, as you may say, a voice was cryin' out, frightened and angry-like; and then Bluff began to bark, bark! Oh, dear! I felt every which way, child. But 't was clear that there was only one path of duty, and that path led through the hole; for a fellow creature was in trouble, and 't was my dog makin' the trouble. Down I went on my face, and through that hole I crawled and wriggled, — don't ask me how, for I don't know to this day, — thinkin' of the sarpent in the Bible all the way.

Suddenly the hole widened, and I found myself in a kind of cave, about five feet by six across, but high enough for me to stand up. I scrambled to my feet, and what should I see but a woman, — a white woman, — sittin' on a heap o' moose and sheep skins, and glarin' at me with eyes like two live coals. She had driven Bluff off, and he stood growlin' in the corner.

For a minute we looked at each other without sayin' anything; I did n't know what upon airth to say. At last she spoke, quite calm, in a deep, strange voice, almost like a man's, but powerful sweet.

"What seek you," she said, " slave? "

Well, that was a queer beginnin', you see, Dolly, and didn't help me much. But I managed to say, "My dog come in, and I followed him — to see what he was barkin' at."

"He was barkin' at me," said the woman. "Bow down before me, slave! I am the Queen!"

And she made a sign with her hand, so commandin'-like that I made a bow, the best way I could. But, of course, I saw then that the poor creature was out of her mind, and I thought 't would be best to humor her, seein' as I had come in without an invitation, as you may say.

"Do you — do you live here, ma'am?" I asked, very polite.

"Your Majesty!" says she, holdin' up her head, and lookin' at me as if I was dirt under her feet.

"Do you live here, your Majesty?" I asked again.

"I am stayin' here," she said. "I am waitin' for the King, who is comin' for me soon. You did not meet him, slave, on your way hither?"

"What king was your Majesty meanin'?" says I.

"King Solomon, of course!" said she. "For what lesser king should the Queen of Sheba wait?"

"To be sure!" says I. "No, ma'am, — your

Majesty, I mean, — I did n't meet King Solomon. I should think you might find a more likely place to wait for him in than this cave. A king would n't be very likely to find his way in here, would he ? "

She looked round with a proud kind o' look. "The chamber is small," she said, " but richly furnished, — richly furnished. You may observe, slave, that the walls are lined with virgin gold."

She waved her hand, and I looked round too at the yellow clay walls and ceilin'. You never could think of such a place, Dolly, unless you 'd ha' seen it. However that poor creature had fixed it up so, no mortal will ever know, I expect. There was a fireplace in one corner, and a hole in the roof over it. I found out arterwards that the smoke went out through a hollow tree that grew right over the cave. There was a fryin'-pan, and some meal in a kind o' bucket made o' birch-bark, some roots, and a few apples. All round the sides she 'd stuck alder-berries and flowers and pine-tassels, and I don't know what not. There was nothin' like a cheer or table, nothin' but the heap o' skins she was settin' on, — that was bed and sofy and everything else for her, I reckon.

And she herself — oh, dear! it makes me want to laugh and cry, both together, to think *how* that unfortinit creature was rigged up. She had a sheepskin over her shoulders, tied round her neck, with the wool outside. On her head was a crown o' birch-bark, cut into p'ints like the crowns in pictures, and stained yeller with the yeller clay, — I suppose she thought it was gold, — and her long black hair was stuck full o' berries and leaves and things. Under the sheepskin she had just nothin' but rags, — such rags as you never seed in all your days, Dolly, your mother bein' the tidy body she is. And moccasins on her feet, — no stockin's; that finished her Majesty's dress. Well, poor soul! and she as proud and contented as you please, fancyin' herself all gold and di'monds.

I made up my mind pretty quick what was the right thing for me to do; and I said, as soothin' as I could, —

" Your Majesty, I don't reelly advise you to wait here no longer for King Solomon. I never seed no kings round these woods, — it 's out o' the line o' kings, as you may say, — and I don't think he 'd be likely to find you out, even if he should stroll down to take a look at the falls, same as I did. Have n't you no other — palace, that's a little more on the travelled road, where he 'd be likely to pass?"

" No," she said, kind o' mournful, and shakin' her head, — " no, slave. I had once, but it was taken from me."

" If you don't mind my bein' so bold," I said, " where was you stayin' before you come here? "

" With devils! " she said, so fierce and sudden that Bluff and I both jumped. " Speak not of them, lest my wrath descend upon you.'"

This was n't very encouragin'; but I was n't a bit frightened, and I set to work again, talkin' and arguin', and kind o' hintin' that there 'd been some kings seen round the place where I lived. That were n't true, o' course, and I knew I was wrong, Dolly, to mislead the poor creature, even if 't was for her good; but I quieted my conscience by thinkin' that 't was true in one way, for Hezekiah King and his nine children lived not more 'n a mile from my house.

Well, to make a long story short, I e'en persuaded the Queen o' Sheba to come home with me, and stay at my house till King Solomon turned up. She did n't much relish the idee of staying with a slave, — as she would have it I was, — but I told her I did n't work for no one but myself, and I was n't no common kind o' slave at all; so at last she give in, poor soul, and followed me as meek as a lamb through the hole, draggin' her big moose-skin — which was her coronation-robe, she said, and she could n't leave it behind — after her, and Bluff growlin' at her heels like all possessed.

Well, I got her home, and gave her some supper, and set her in a cheer; and you never in all your life see any one so pleased. She looked, and looked, and you 'd ha' thought this kitchen was Marble Halls like them in the song. It *did* look cheerful and pleasant, but much the same as it does now, after sixty years, little Dolly. And if you 'll believe it, it 's this very arm-cheer as I 'm sittin' in now, that the Queen o' Sheba sot in. It had a flowered chintz cover then, new and bright. Well, she sat back at last, and drew a long breath.

" You have done well, faithful slave ! " she said. "This is my own palace that you have brought me to. I know it well, — well; and this is my throne, from which I shall judge the people till the King comes."

This is what the boys would call "rather cool;" but I only said, "Yes, your Majesty, you shall judge every one there is to judge," — which was me and Bluff, and Crummy the cow, and ten fowls, and the pig. She was just as pleasant and condescendin' as could be all the evenin', and when I put her to bed in the fourposter in the spare room, she praised me again, and said that when the King came she would give me a carcanet of rubies, whatever that is.

Just as soon as she was asleep, the first thing that I did was to open the stove and put her rags in, piece by piece, till they was all burnt up. The moose-skin, which was a good one, I hung out on the line to air. Then I brought out some clothes of Mother's that I 'd kep' laid away, — a good calico dress and some underclothing, all nice and fresh, — and laid them over the back of a cheer by her bed. It seemed kind o' strange to go to bed with a ravin' lunatic, as you may say, in the next room ; but I knew I was doin' right, and that was all there was to it. The Lord would see to the rest, I thought.

Next mornin' I was up bright and early, and soon as I'd made the fire and tidied up and got breakfast under way, I went in to see how her Majesty was. She was wide awake, sittin' up in bed, and lookin' round her as wild as a hawk. Seemed as if she was just goin' to spring out o' bed; but when she saw me, she quieted down, and when I spoke easy and soothin' like, and asked her how she'd slept, she answered pleasant enough.

"But where are my robes?" said she, pointin' to the clothes I'd laid out. "Those are not my robes."

"They's new robes," I said, quite bold. "The old ones had to be taken away, your Majesty. They were n't fit for you to wear, really,—all but the coronation robe; and that's hangin' on the line, to — to take the wrinkles out."

Well, I had a hard fight over the clothes; she could n't make up her mind nohow to put 'em on. But at last I had an idee. "Don't you know," I said, "the Bible says 'The King's Daughter is all radiant within, in raiment of wrought needle-work'? Well, this is wrought needlework, every bit of it."

I showed her the seams and the stitches; and, my dear, she put it on without another word, and was as pleased as Punch when she was dressed up all neat and clean. Then I brushed her hair out, — lovely hair it was, comin' down below her knees, and thick enough for a cloak, but matted and tangled so 't was a sight to behold, — and braided it, and put it up on top of her head like a sort o' crown, and I tell you she looked like a queen, if ever anybody did. She fretted a little for her birch-bark crown, but I told her how Scripture said a woman's glory was her hair, and that quieted her at once. Poor soul! she was real good and pious, and she 'd listen to Scripture readin' by the hour; but I allus had to wind up with somethin' about King Solomon.

Well, Dolly, the Queen o' Sheba stayed with me (I must make my story short, Honey, for your ma 'll be comin' for ye soon now) three years; and I will say that they was happy years for both of us. Not yourself could be more biddable than that poor crazy Queen was, once she got wonted to me and the place. At first she was inclined to wander off, a-lookin' for the King; but bimeby she got into the way of occupyin' herself, spinnin'

— she was a beautiful spinner, and when I told her 't was Scriptural, I could hardly get her away from the wheel — and trimmin' the house up with flowers, and playin' with Bluff, for all the world like a child. And in the evenin's, — well, there! she 'd sit on her throne and tell stories about her kingdom, and her gold and spices, and myrrh and frankincense and things, and all the great things she was goin' to do for her faithful slave, — that was me, ye know; she never would call me anything else, — till it all seemed just as good as true. *'T was* true to her; and if 't had been really true for me, I should n't ha' been half so well off as in my own sp'ere; so 't was all right.

My dear, my poor Queen might have been with me to this day, if it had n't been for the meddlesomeness of men. I 've heerd talk o' women meddling, and very likely they may, when they live along o' men; but it don't begin with women, nor yet end with 'em. One day I 'd been out 'tendin' to the cow, and as I was comin' back I heerd screams and shrieks, and a man's voice talkin' loud. You may believe I run, Dolly, as fast as run I could; and when I came to the kitchen there was Hezekiah King and a strange man standin' and talkin' to the Queen. She was all in a heap behind the big chair, poor soul, tremblin' like a leaf, and her eyes glarin' like they did the fust time I see her; and she did n't say a word, only scream, like a panther in a trap, every minute or two.

I steps before her, and " What 's this? " says I, short enough.

" Mornin', Ca-iry," says Hezekiah, smilin' his greasy smile, that allus *did* make me want to slap his face. " This is Mr. Clamp, from Coptown. Make ye acquainted with Miss Ca-iry Pennypacker, Mr. Clamp. I met up with Mr. Clamp yesterday, Ca-iry, and I was tellin' him about this demented creatur as you 've been shelterin' at your own expense the last three years, as the hull neighborhood says it 's a shame. And lo! how myster'ous is the ways o' Providence! Mr. Clamp is sup'n'tendent o' the Poor Farm down to Coptown, and he says this woman is a crazy pauper as he has had in keer for six year, ever since she lost her wits along o' her husband bein' drownded. She run away three year ago last spring, and he ain't heard nothin' of her till yisterday, when he just chanced to meet up with me. So now he's come as in dooty bound, she belongin' to the deestrick o' Coptown, to take her off your hands, and thank ye for — "

He had n't no time to say more. I took him by the shoulders, — I was mortal strong in those days, Dolly; there was n't a man within ten miles but I could ha' licked him if he 'd been wuth it, — and shot him out o' the door like a sack o' flour. Then I took the other man, who was standin' with his mouth open, for all the world like a codfish, and shot him out arter him. He tumbled against Hezekiah, and they both went down together, and sat there and looked at me with their mouths open.

" You go home," says I, " and take care o' your-selves, if you know how. When I want you or the like o' you, I 'll send for you. *Scat!* " And I shut the door and bolted it, b'ilin' with rage, and came back to my poor Queen.

She was down on the floor, all huddled up in a corner, moanin' and moanin', like a dumb beast that has a death wound. I lifted her up, and tried to soothe and quiet her, — she was tremblin' all over, — but 't was hard work. Not a word could I get

out of her but " Devil! Devil!" and then " Solomon!" over and over again. I brought the Bible,
and read her about the Temple, and the knops and
the flowers, and the purple, and the gold dishes, till
she was quiet again ; and then I put her to bed,
poor soul! though 't was only six o'clock, and sat
and sang " Jerusalem the Golden " till she dropped
off to sleep. I was b'ilin' mad still, and besides I
was afraid she 'd have a fit o' sickness, or turn
ravin', after the fright, so I did n't sleep much
myself that night. Towards mornin', however, I
dropped off, and must have slept sound ; for when
I woke it was seven o'clock, the sun was up high,
the door was swingin' open, and the Queen o'
Sheba was gone.

Don't ask me, little Dolly, how I felt, when I
found that poor creature was nowhere on the
place. I knew where to go, though. Something
told me, plain as words ; and Bluff and I, we made
a bee-line for the Rollin' Dam woods. The dog
found her first. She had tried to get into her hole,
but the earth had caved in over it ; so she had laid
down beside it, on the damp ground, in her night-
gown. Oh, dear! oh, dear! How long she 'd
been there, nobody will ever know. She was in a

kind o' swoon, and I had to carry her most o' the way, however I managed to do it; but I was mortal strong in those days, and she was slight and light, for all her bein' tall. When I got her home and laid her in her bed, I knowed she 'd never leave it; and sure enough, before night she was in a ragin' fever. A week it lasted; and when it began to go down, her life went with it. My poor Queen! she was real gentle when the fiery heat was gone. She lay there like a child, so weak and white. One night, when I 'd been singin' to her a spell, she took this little bag from her neck, where she 'd allus worn it, under her clothes, and giv' it to me.

"Faithful slave," she said, — she could n't speak above a whisper, — "King Solomon is comin' for me to-night. I have had a message from him. I leave you this as a token of my love and gratitude. It is the Great Talisman, more precious than gold or gems. Open it when I am gone. And now, good slave, kiss me, for I would sleep awhile."

I kissed my poor dear, and she dozed off peaceful and happy. But all of a sudden she opened her eyes with a start, and sat up in the bed.

"Solomon!" she cried, and held out her arms

wide. "Solomon, my King!" and then fell back on the piller, dead.

There, little Dolly! don't you cry, dear! 'T was the best thing for the poor thing. I opened the bag, when it was all over, and what do you think I found? A newspaper slip, sayin', "Lost at sea, on March 2, 18—, Solomon Marshall, twenty-seven years," and a lock o' dark-brown hair. Them was the Great Talisman. But if true love and faith can make a thing holy, this poor little bag is holy, and as such I 've kept it.

There 's your ma comin', Dolly. Put on your bonnet, Honey, quick! And see here, dear! you need n't tell her nothin' I said about Hezekiah King. I clean forgot he was your grandfather.

CHAPTER VIII.

FLOWER-DAY.

"Cousin Wealthy," said Hildegarde at breakfast the next morning, "may I tell you what it was that made me so rude as to interrupt you last night?"

"Certainly, my dear," said Miss Wealthy; "you may tell me, and then you may forget the little accident, as I had already done."

"Well," said Hildegarde, "you spoke of the time when Mamma was a 'harum-scarum girl;' and the idea of her ever having been anything of the sort was so utterly amazing that — that was why I cried out. Is it possible that Mammy was not always quiet and blessed and peaceful?"

"Mildred!" exclaimed Miss Wealthy. "Mildred peaceful! My *dear* Hilda!"

An impressive pause followed, and Hildegarde's eyes began to twinkle. "Tell us!" she murmured, in a tone that would have persuaded an oyster to open his shell. Then she stroked Miss Wealthy's arm gently, and was silent, for she saw that speech was coming in due time.

Miss Wealthy looked at her teacup, and shook her head slowly, smiled, and then sighed. "Mildred!" she said again. "My dear, your mother is now forty years old, and I am seventy. When she came to visit me for the first time, *I* was forty years old, and she was ten. She had on, when she arrived, a gray stuff frock, trimmed with many rows of narrow green braid, and a little gray straw bonnet, with rows of quilled satin ribbon, green and pink." The girls exchanged glances of horror and amazement at the thought of this headgear, but made no sound. "I shall never forget that bonnet," continued Miss Wealthy, pensively, "nor that dress. In getting out of the carriage her skirt caught on the step, and part of a row of braid was ripped; this made a loop, in which she caught her foot, and tumbled headlong to the ground. I mended it in the evening, after she was in bed, as it was the frock she was to wear every morning. My dears, I mended that frock every day for a month. It is the truth! the braid caught on everything, — on latches, on brambles, on pump-handles, on posts, on chairs. There was always a loop of it hanging, and the child was always putting her foot through it and tumbling down. She never cried, though sometimes, when she fell downstairs, she must have hurt herself. A very brave little girl she was. At last I took all the braid off, and then things went a little better."

Miss Wealthy paused to sip her coffee, and Hildegarde tried not to look as if she begrudged her the sip. "Then," she went on, "Mildred was always running away, — not intentionally, you understand, but just going off and forgetting to come back. Once — dear, dear! it gives me a turn to think of it! — she had been reading 'Neighbor Jackwood,' and was much delighted with the idea of the heroine's hiding in the haystack to escape her cruel pursuers. So she went out to the great haystack in the barnyard, pulled out a quantity of hay, crept into the hole, and found it so comfortable that she fell fast asleep. You may imagine, my dears, what my feelings were when dinner-time came, and Mildred was not to be found. The house was searched from garret to cellar. Martha and I — Martha had just come to me then — went down to the wharf and through the orchard and round by the pasture, calling and calling, till our throats were sore. At last, as no trace of the child could be found, I made up my mind that she must have wandered away into the woods and got lost. It was a terrible thought, my dears! I called Enoch, the man, and bade him saddle the horse and ride round to call out the neighbors, that they might all search together. As he was leading the horse out, he noticed a quantity of hay on the ground, and wondered how it had come there. Coming nearer, he saw the hole in the stack, looked in, and — there was the child, fast asleep!"

"Oh! naughty little mother!" cried Hildegarde. "What did you do to her, Cousin Wealthy?"

"Nothing, my dear," replied the good lady. "I was quite ill for several days from the fright, and that was enough punishment for the poor child. She never *meant* to be naughty, you know. But my heart was in my mouth all the time. Once, coming home from a walk, I heard a cheery little voice crying, 'Cousin Wealthy! Cousin! see where I am!' I looked up. Hilda, she was sitting on the ridge-pole of the house, waving her bonnet by a loop of the pink quilled ribbon, — it was almost as bad as the green braid about coming off, — and smiling like a cherub. "I came through the skylight," she said, "and the air up here is *so* fresh and nice! I wish you would come up, Cousin!"

Another time — oh, that was the worst time of all! I really thought I should die that time." Miss Wealthy paused, and shook her head.

"Oh, do go on, dear!" cried Hildegarde; "unless you are tired, that is. It is *so* delightful!"

"It was anything but delightful for me, my dear, I can assure you," rejoined Miss Wealthy.

"This happened several years later, when Mildred was thirteen or fourteen. She came to me for a winter visit, and I was delighted to find how womanly she had grown. We had a great deal of bad weather, and she was with me in the house a good deal, and was most sweet and helpful; and as I did not go out much, I did not see what she did out of doors, and she *always* came home in time for dinner and tea. Well, one day — it was in March, and the river was just breaking up, as we had had some mild weather — the minister came to see me, and I began to tell him about Mildred, and how she had developed, and how much comfort I took in her womanly ways. He was sitting on the sofa, from which, you know, one can see the river very well. Suddenly he said, " Dear me! what is that? Some one on the river at this time! Very imprudent! Very — " Then he broke off short, and gave me a strange look.

I sprang up and went to the window. What did I see, my dear girls? The river was full of great cakes of ice, all pressed and jumbled together; the current was running very swiftly; and there, in the middle of the river, jumping from one cake to another like a chamois, or some such wild creature, was Mildred Bond."

"Oh!" cried Rose, "how dreadful! Dear Miss Bond, what did you do?"

Hildegarde was silent. It was certainly very naughty, she thought; but oh, what fun it must have been!

"Fortunately," said Miss Wealthy, "I became quite faint at the sight. Fortunately, I say; for I might have screamed and startled the child, and made her lose her footing. As it was, the minister went and called Martha, and she, like the sensible girl she is, simply blew the dinner-horn as loud as she possibly could. It was the middle of the afternoon; but as she rightly conjectured, the sound, without startling Mildred, gave her to understand that she was wanted. The minister watched her making her way to the shore, leaping the dark spaces of rushing water between the cakes, apparently as unconcerned as if she were walking along the highway; and when he saw her safe on shore, he was very glad to sit down and drink a glass of the wine that Martha had brought to revive me. 'My dear madam,' he said, — I was lying on the sofa in dreadful suspense, and could not trust myself to look, — 'the young lady is safe on the bank, and will be here in a moment. I fear she is not so sedate as you fancied; and as she is too old to be spanked and put to bed, I should recommend your sending her home by the coach to-morrow morning. That girl, madam, needs the curb, and you have been guiding her with the snaffle.' He was very fond of horses, good-man, and always drove a good one himself."

"And did you send her home?" asked Hildegarde, anxiously, thinking what a dreadful thing it would be to be sent back in disgrace.

"Oh, no!" said Miss Wealthy, "I could not do that, of course. Mildred was my god-child, and I loved her dearly. But she was not allowed to see me for twenty-four hours, and I fancy those were very sad hours for her. Dear Mildred! that was her last prank; for the next time she came here she was a woman grown, and all the hoyden ways had been put off like a garment. And now, dears," added Miss Wealthy, rising, "we must let Martha take these dishes, or she will be late with her work, and that always distresses her extremely."

They went into the parlor, and Hildegarde, as she patted and "plumped" the cushions of the old lady's chair, reminded her that she had promised them some work for the morning, but had not told them what it was.

"True!" said Miss Wealthy. "You are right, dear. This is my Flower-day. I send flowers once a week to the sick children in the hospital at Fairtown, and I thought you might like to pick them and make up the nosegays."

"Oh, how delightful that will be!" cried Hildegarde. "And is that what you call work, Cousin Wealthy? I call it play, and the best kind. We must go at once, so as to have them all picked before the sun is hot. Come, Rosebud!"

The girls put on their broad-brimmed hats and went out into the garden, which was still cool and dewy. Jeremiah was there, of course, with his wheelbarrow; and as

they stood looking about them, Martha appeared with a tray in one hand and a large
shallow tin box in the other. Waving the
tray as a signal to the girls to follow, she
led the way to a shady corner, where, under
a drooping laburnum-tree, was a table and
a rustic seat. She set the tray and box
on the table, and then, diving into her
capacious pocket, produced a ball of string,
two pairs of flower-scissors, and a roll of
tissue paper.

"There!" she said, in a tone of satisfaction, "I think that's all. Pretty work
you'll find it, Miss Hilda, and it's right
glad I am to have you do it; for it is too
much for Miss Bond, stooping over the
beds, so it is. But do it she will; and I
almost think she hardly liked to give it
up, even to you."

"Indeed, I don't wonder!" said Hildegarde. "There cannot be anything else so

PREPARING FOR FLOWER-DAY.

pleasant to do. And thank you, Martha, for making everything so comfortable for us. You are a dear, as I may have said before."

Martha chuckled and withdrew, after telling the girls that the flowers must be ready in an hour.

"Now, Rose," said Hildegarde, "you will sit there and arrange the pretty dears as I bring them to you. The question is now, where to begin. I never, in all my life, saw so many flowers!"

"Begin with those that will not crush easily," said Rose, "and I will lay them at the bottom. Some of those splendid sweet-williams over there, and mignonette, and calendula, and sweet alyssum, and—"

"Oh, certainly!" cried Hildegarde. "All at once, of course, picking with all my hundred hands at the same moment. Could n't you name a few more, Miss?"

"I beg pardon!" said Rose, laughing. "I will confine my attention to the laburnum here. 'Allee same,' I don't believe you see that beautiful mourning-bride behind you."

"Why mourning, and why bride?" asked Hildegarde, plucking some of the dark, rich blossoms. "It does n't strike me as a melancholy flower."

"I don't know!" said Rose. "I used to play that she was a princess, and so wore crimson instead of black for mourning. She is so beautiful, it is a pity she has no fragrance. She is of the teasel family, you know."

"Lady Teazle?" asked Hildegarde, laughing.

"A different branch!" replied Rose, "but just as prickly. The fuller's teasel, — do you know about it, dear?"

"No, Miss Encyclopædia, I do not!" replied Hildegarde, with some asperity. "You know I *never* know anything of that kind; tell me about it!"

"Well, it is very curious," said Rose, taking the great bunch of mourning-bride that her friend handed her, and separating the flowers daintily. "The flower-heads of this teasel, when they are dried, are covered with sharp curved hooks, and are used to raise the nap on woollen cloth. No machine or instrument that can be invented does it half so well as this dead and withered blossom. Is n't that interesting?"

"Very!" said Hildegarde. "Oh, dear! oh, dear!"

"What *is* the matter?" cried Rose, in alarm. "Has something stung you? Let me —"

"Oh, no!" said Hildegarde, quickly. "I was only thinking of the appalling number of things there are to know. They overwhelm me! They bury me! A mountain weighs me down, and on its top grows a — a teasel. Why,

I never heard of the thing! I am not sure that I am clear what a fuller is, except that his earth is advertised in the Pears' soap-boxes."

They both laughed at this, and then Hildegarde bent with renewed energy over a bed of feathered pinks of all shades of crimson and rose-color.

"A mountain!" said Rose, slowly and thoughtfully, as she laid the blossoms together and tied them up in small posies. "Yes, Hilda, so it is! but a mountain to climb, not to be buried under. To think that we can go on climbing, learning, all our lives, and always with higher and higher peaks above us, soaring up and up, — oh, it is glorious! What might be the matter with you to-day, my lamb?" she added; for Hildegarde groaned, and plunged her face into a great white lily, withdrawing it to show a nose powdered with virgin gold. "Does your head ache?"

"I think the sturgeon is at the bottom of it," was the reply. "I have not yet recovered fully from the humiliation of having been so frightened by a sturgeon, when I had been brought up, so to speak, on the 'Culprit Fay.' I have eaten caviare too," she added gloomily, — " odious stuff!"

"But, my *dear* Hilda!" cried Rose, in amused perplexity, " this is too absurd. Why shouldn't one be frightened at a monstrous creature leaping out of the water just before one's nose, and how should you know he was a sturgeon? You couldn't expect him to say 'I am a sturgeon!' or to carry a placard hung round his neck, with 'Fresh Caviare!' on it." Hildegarde laughed. " You remind me," added Rose, "that my own ignorance list is getting pretty long. Get me some sweet-peas, that's a dear; and I can ask you the things while you are picking them." Hildegarde moved to the long rows of sweet-peas, which grew near the laburnum bower; and Rose drew a little brown note-book from her pocket, and laid it open on the table beside her. "What is 'Marlowe's mighty line'?" she demanded bravely. "I keep coming across the quotation in different things, and I don't know who Marlowe was. Yet you see I am cheerful."

"Kit Marlowe!" said Hildegarde. "Poor Kit! he was a great dramatist; the next greatest after Shakspeare, I think, — at least, well, leaving out the Greeks, you know. He was a year younger than Shakspeare, and died when he was only twenty-eight, killed in a tavern brawl."

"Oh, how dreadful!" cried gentle Rose. "Then he had only begun to write."

"Oh, no!" said Hildegarde. "He had written a great deal, — 'Faustus' and 'Edward II.,' and 'Tamburlaine,' and — oh! I don't know all. But one thing of his *you* know, 'The Passionate Shepherd,' — 'Come live with me and be my love;' you remember?"

"Oh!" cried Rose. "Did he write that? I love him, then."

"And so many, many lovely things!" continued Hildegarde, warming to her subject, and snipping sweet-peas vigorously. "Mamma has read me a good deal here and there, — all of 'Edward II.,' and bits from 'Faustus.' There is one place, where he sees Helen — oh, I must remember it! —

"'Was this the face that launched a thousand ships,
   And burnt the topless towers of Ilium?'

Isn't that full of pictures? I see them! I see the ships, and the white, royal city, and the beautiful, beautiful face looking down from a tower window."

Both girls were silent a moment; then Rose asked timidly, "And who spoke of the 'mighty line,' dear? It must have been another great poet. Only three words, and such a roll and ring and brightness in them."

"Oh! Ben Jonson!" said Hildegarde. "He was another great dramatist, you know; a little younger, but of the same time with Shakspeare and Marlowe. He lived to be quite old, and he wrote a very famous poem on Shakspeare, ' all full of quotations,' as somebody said about 'Hamlet.' It is in that that he says 'Marlowe's mighty line,' and 'Sweet Swan of Avon,' and 'Soul of the Age,' and all sorts of pleasant things. So nice of him!"

"And — and was he an ancestor of Dr. Samuel's?" asked Rose, humbly.

"Why, darling, you are really quite ignorant!" cried Hildegarde, laughing. "How delightful to find things that you don't know! No, he had no *h* in his name, — at least, it had been left out; but he came originally from the Johnstones of Annandale. Think of it! he may have been a cousin of Jock Johnstone the Tinkler, without knowing it. Well, his father died when he was little, and his mother married a bricklayer; and Ben used to carry hods of mortar up ladders, — oh me'! what a strange world it is! By-and-by he was made Laureate, — the first Laureate, — and he was very great and glorious, and wrote masques and plays and poems, and quarrelled with Inigo Jones — no! I can't stop to tell you who he was," seeing the question in Rose's eyes, — "and grew very fat. But when he was old they neglected him, poor dear! and when he died he was buried standing up straight, in Westminster Abbey; and his friend Jack Young paid a workman eighteenpence to carve on a stone ' O Rare Ben Jonson!' and there it is to this day."

She paused for breath; but Rose said nothing, seeing that more was coming. "But the best of all," continued Hildegarde, "was his visit to Drummond of Hawthornden. Oh, Rose, that was so delightful!"

"Tell me about it!" said Rose, softly. "Not that I know who *he* was; but his name is a poem in itself."

"Is n't it?" cried Hildegarde. "He was a poet too, a Scottish poet, living in a wonderful old house —"

"Not 'caverned Hawthornden,' in 'Lovely Rosabelle'?" cried Rose, her eyes lighting up with new interest.

"Yes!" replied Hildegarde, "just that. Do you know why it is 'caverned'? That must be another story. Remind me to tell you when we are doing our hair to-night. But now you must hear about Ben. Well, he went on a walking tour to Scotland, and one of his first visits was to William Drummond, with whom he had corresponded a good deal. Drummond was sitting under his great sycamore-tree, waiting for him, and at last he saw a great ponderous figure coming down the avenue, flourishing a huge walking-stick. Of course he knew who it was; so he went forward to meet him, and called out, ' Welcome, welcome, royal Ben!' ' Thank ye, thank ye, Hawthornden!' answered Jonson; and then they both laughed and were friends at once."

" Hildegarde, where do you find all these wonderful things?" cried Rose, in amazement. " That is delightful, enchanting. And for you to call yourself ignorant! Oh!"

"There is a life of Drummond at home," said Hildegarde, simply. " Of course one reads lovely things, — there is no merit in that; and the teasel still flaunts. But I *do* feel better. That is just my baseness, to be glad when you don't know things, you dearest! But do just look at these sweet-peas! I have picked all these, — pecks! bushels! — and there are as many as ever. Don't you think we have enough flowers, Rosy?"

"I do indeed!" answered Rose. "Enough for a hundred children at least. Besides, it must be time for them to go. The lovely things! Think of all the pleasure they will give! A sick child, and a bunch of flowers like these!" She took up a posy of velvet pansies and sweet-peas, set round with mignonette, and put it lovingly to her lips. "I remember —" She paused, and sighed, and then smiled.

"Yes, dear!" said Hildegarde, interrogatively. "The house where you were born?"

"One day I was in dreadful pain," said Rose, — "pain that seemed as if it would never end, · — and a little child from a neigh-bor's house brought a bunch of Ragged

Robin, and laid it on my pillow, and said, 'Poor Pinky! make she better!' I think I have never loved any other flower quite so much as Ragged Robin, since then. It is the only one I miss here. Do you want to hear the little rhyme I made about it, when I was old enough?"

Hildegarde answered by sitting down on the arm of the rustic seat, and throwing her arm round her friend's shoulder in her favorite fashion. "Such a pleasant Rose-bud!" she murmured. "Tell now!"

And Rose told about —

RAGGED ROBIN.

O Robin, ragged Robin,
  That stands beside the door,
The sweetheart of the country child,
  The flower of the poor,

I love to see your cheery face,
  Your straggling bravery;
Than many a stately garden bloom
  You 're dearer far to me.

For you it needs no sheltered nook,
  No well-kept flower-bed;
By cottage porch, by roadside ditch,
  You raise your honest head.

The small hedge-sparrow knows you well,
  The blackbird is your friend;
With clustering bees and butterflies
  Your pink-fringed blossoms bend.

O Robin, ragged Robin,
  The dearest flower that grows,
Why don't you patch your tattered cloak?
  Why don't you mend your hose?

Would you not like to prank it there
  Within the border bright,
Among the roses and the pinks,
  A courtly dame's delight?

"Ah no!" says jolly Robin,
  "'T would never do for me;
The friend of bird and butterfly,
  Like them I must be free.

" The garden is for stately folk,
  The lily and the rose;
They 'd scorn my coat of ragged pink,
  Would flout my broken hose.

" Then let me bloom in wayside ditch,
     And by the cottage door,
The sweetheart of the country child,
     The flower of the poor."

CHAPTER IX.

BROKEN FLOWERS.

Miss Wealthy was sitting on the back piazza, crocheting a tidy. The stitch was a new one, and quite complicated, and her whole mind was bent upon it. "One, two, purl, chain, slip; one, two, purl" — when suddenly descended upon her a whirlwind, a vision of sparkling eyes and "tempestuous petticoat," crying, "*Please*, Cousin Wealthy, may I go with Jeremiah? The wagon is all ready. May n't I go? Oh, *please* say 'yes'!"

Miss Wealthy started so violently that the crochet-hook fell from her hands. "My *dear* Hilda!" she said plaintively, "you quite take my breath away. I — really, my dear, I don't know what to say. Where do you want to go?"

"With Jeremiah, to Fairtown, with the flowers — to see the children!" cried Hildegarde, still too much out of breath to speak connectedly, but dropping on one knee beside the old lady, and stroking her soft hand apologetically. "He says he will take care of me; and Rose has a long letter to write, and I shall be back in time for dinner. Dear, nice, pretty, sweet, bewitching Cousin Wealthy, may I go?"

Miss Wealthy was still bewildered. "Why, my dear," she said hesitatingly. "Yes — you may go, certainly — if you are quite sure — "

But Hildegarde waited for no "ifs." She whirled upstairs, flew out of her pink gingham and into a sober dark blue one, exchanged her garden hat for a blue "sailor,"

whirled downstairs again, kissed Rose on
both cheeks, dropped another kiss on Miss
Wealthy's cap, and was in the wagon and
out of sight round the corner before any one
with moderately deliberate enunciation could
have said " Jack Robinson."

Miss Wealthy dropped back in her chair,
and drew a long, fluttering breath. She
looked flushed and worried, and put her hand
nervously up to the pansy brooch. Seeing
this, Rose came quietly, picked up the crochet-
hook, and sat down to admire the work, and
wonder if she could learn the stitch. " Perhaps some time you would show it to me,
dear Miss Bond," she said ; " and now may
I read you that article on window-gardening
that you said you would like to hear ? "

So Rose read, in her low, even tones,
smooth and pleasant as the rippling of
water ; and Miss Wealthy's brow grew calm
again, and the flush passed away, and her

thoughts passed pleasantly from " one, two, purl, slip," to gloxinias and cyclamen, and back again; till at length, the day being warm, she fell asleep, which was exactly what the wily Rose meant her to do.

Meantime Hildegarde was speeding along toward the station, seated beside Jeremiah in the green wagon, with the box of flowers stowed safely under the seat. She was in high spirits, and determined to enjoy every moment of her " escapade," as she called it. Jeremiah surveyed her bright face with chastened melancholy.

" Reckon you're in for a junket," he said kindly. " Quite a head o' steam you carry. 'T'll do ye good to work it off some."

" Yes!" cried Hildegarde. " It is a regular frolic, isn't it, Jeremiah? How beautiful everything looks! What a perfection of a day it is!"

"Fine hayin' weather!" Jeremiah assented. "We sh'll begin to-morrow, I calc'late. Pleasant, hayin' time is. Now, thar's a field!" He pointed with his whip to a broad meadow all blue-green with waving timothy, and sighed, and shook his head.

"Is n't·it a good field?" asked Hildegarde, innocently.

"Best lot on the place!" replied the prophet, with melancholy enthusiasm. "Not many lots like that in *this* neighborhood! There's a power o' grass there. Well, sirs! grass must be cut, and hay must be eat, — there's no gainsayin' that, — 'in the sweat o' thy brow,' ye understand; but still there's some enj'yment in it."

Hildegarde could not quite follow this sentence, which seemed to be only half addressed to her; so she only nodded sagely, and turned her attention to the ferns by the roadside.

It was less than an hour's trip to Fairtown, nor was the walk long through the pleasant, elm-shaded streets. The hospital was a brick building, painted white, and looking very neat and trim, with its striped awnings, and its flagged pathway between rows of box. One saw that it had been a fine dwelling-house in its day, for the wood of the doorway was cunningly carved, and the brass knocker was quite a work of art.

Jeremiah knocked; and when the door was opened by a neat maidservant, he brought the box of flowers, and laid it on a table in the hall. "Miss Bond's niece!" he said, with a nod of explanation and introduction. "Thought she'd come herself; like to see the young ones. I'll be back for ye in an hour," he added to Hildegarde, and with another nod departed.

After waiting a few minutes in a cool, shady parlor, where she sat feeling strange and shy, and wishing she had not come, Hildegarde was greeted by a sweet-faced woman in spotless cap and apron, who bade her welcome, and asked for Miss Bond. "It is some time since she has been here!" she added. "We are always so glad to see her, dear lady. But her kindness comes every week in the lovely flowers, and the children do think so much of them. Would you like to distribute them yourself to-day? A new face is always a pleasure, if it is a kind one; and yours will bring sunshine, I am sure."

"Oh, thank you!" said Hildegarde, shyly. "It is just what I wanted, if you really think they would like it."

Mrs. Murray, as the matron was called, seemed to have no doubt upon this point, and led the way upstairs, the servant following with the flowers. She opened a door, and led Hildegarde into a large, sunny room, with little white beds all along the wall. On every pillow lay a little head ; and many faces turned toward the opening door, with a look of pleasure at meeting the matron's cheery smile. Hildegarde opened her great box, and taking up three or four bouquets, moved forward hesitatingly. This was something new to her. She had visited girls of her own age or more, in the New York hospitals, but she was not used to little children, being herself an only child. In the first cot lay a little girl, a mite of five years, with a pale patient face. She could not move her hands, but she turned her face toward the bunch of sweet-peas that Hildegarde laid on the pillow, and murmured, "Pitty! pitty!"

"Are n't they sweet?" said Hildegarde. "Do you see that they have little wings, almost like butterflies ? When the wind blows, they flutter about, and seem to be alive, almost."

The child smiled, and put her lips to the cool fragrant blossoms. "Kiss butterf'ies!" she said; and at this Hildegarde kissed her, and went on to the next crib.

Here lay a child of seven, her sweet blue eyes heavy with fever, her cheeks flushed and burning. She stretched out her hands toward the flowers, and said, "White ones! give me white ones, Lady! Red ones is hot! Minnie is too hot. White ones is cold."

A nurse stood beside the crib, and Hildegarde looked to her for permission, then filled the little hands with sweet alyssum and white roses.

"The roses were all covered with dew when I picked them," she said softly. "See, dear, they are still cool and fresh." And she laid them against the burning cheek. "There was a great bed of roses in a lovely garden, and while I was at one end of it, a little humming-bird came to the other, and hovered about, and put his bill into the flowers. His head was bright green, like the leaves, and his throat was ruby-red, and — "

" Guess that's a lie, ain't it ? " asked the child, wearily.

" Oh, no ! " said Hildegarde, smiling. " It is all true, every word. When you are better, I will send you a picture of a humming-bird."

She nodded kindly, and moved on, to give red roses to a bright little tot in a red flannel dressing-gown, who was sitting up in bed, nursing a rubber elephant. He took the roses and said, " Sanks ! " very politely, then held them to his pet's gray proboscis. " I 's better," he explained, with some condescension. " I don't need 'em, but Nelephant doos. He's a severe case. Doctor said so vis mornin'."

" Indeed ! " said Hildegarde, sympathetically. "I am very sorry. What is the matter with him?"

"Mumps 'n' ague 'n' brown kitties 'n' ammonia 'n' fits!" was the prompt reply; "and a hole in his leg too! Feel his pult!"

He held up a gray leg, which Hildegarde examined gravely. "It seems to be hollow," she said. "Did the doctor think that was a bad sign?"

"It's fits," said the child, "or a brown kitty, — I don't know which. Is you a nurse?"

"No, dear," said Hildegarde; "I only came to bring the flowers. I must go away soon, but I shall think of you and the elephant, and I hope he will be better soon."

"Sing!" was the unexpected reply, in a tone of positive command.

"Benny!" said Mrs. Murray, who came up at this moment; "you must n't tease the

"'FEEL HIS PULT,' SAID BENNY."

young lady, dear. See! the other children are waiting for their flowers, and you have these lovely roses."

"She looks singy!" persisted Benny. "I wants her to sing. Doctor said I could have what I wanted, and I wants *vat*."

"May I sing to him?" asked Hildegarde, in a low tone. "I can sing a little, if it would not disturb the others."

But Mrs. Murray thought the others would like it very much. So Hildegarde first gave posies to all the other children in the room, and then came back and sat down on Benny's bed, and sang, "Up the airy mountain," in a very sweet, clear voice. Several little ones had been tossing about in feverish restlessness, but now they lay still and listened; and when the song was over, a hoarse voice from a corner of the room cried, "More! more sing!"

"She's *my* more! she isn't your more!"

cried Benny, sitting erect, with flashing eyes that glared across the room at the offender. But a soft hand held a cup of milk to his lips, and laid him back on the pillow; and the nurse motioned to Hildegarde to go on.

Then she sang, " Ring, ting! I wish I were a primrose; " and then another of dear William Allingham's, which had been her own pet song when she was Benny's age.

> "'Oh, birdie, birdie, will you, pet?
> Summer is far and far away yet.
> You'll get silken coats and a velvet bed,
> And a pillow of satin for your head.'

> "'I'd rather sleep in the ivy wall!
> No rain comes through, though I hear it fall.
> The sun peeps gay at dawn of day,
> And I sing and wing away, away.'

> "'Oh, birdie, birdie, will you, pet?
> Diamond stones, and amber and jet,
> I'll string in a necklace fair and fine,
> To please this pretty bird of mine.'

"'Oh, thanks for diamonds and thanks for jet,
  But here is something daintier yet.
  A feather necklace round and round,
  That I would not sell for a thousand pound.'

"'Oh, birdie, birdie, won't you, pet?
  I'll buy you a dish of silver fret;
  A golden cup and an ivory seat,
  And carpets soft beneath your feet.'

"'Can running water be drunk from gold?
  Can a silver dish the forest hold?
  A rocking twig is the finest chair,
  And the softest paths lie through the air.
  Farewell, farewell to my lady fair!'"

By the time the song was finished, Benny was sleeping quietly, and the nurse thanked Hildegarde for "getting him off so cleverly. He needed a nap," she said; "and if he thinks we want him to go to sleep, he sets all his little strength against it. He's getting better, the lamb!"

"What has been the matter?" asked Hildegarde.

"Pneumonia," was the reply. "He has come out of it very well, but I dread the day when he must go home to a busy, careless mother and a draughty cottage. He ought to have a couple of weeks in the country."

At this moment the head nurse — a tall, slender woman with a beautiful face — came from an inner room, the door of which had been standing ajar. She held out her hand to Hildegarde, and the girl saw that her eyes were full of tears. "Thank you," she said, "for the song. Another little bird has just flown away from earth, and he went smiling, when he heard you sing. Have you any sweet little flowers, pink and white?"

The quick tears sprang to Hilda's eyes. She could not speak for a moment, but she lifted some lovely sprays of blush rosebuds, which the nurse took with a smile and a look of thanks. The girl's eyes followed her; and before the door closed she caught a glimpse of a little still form, and a cloud of fair curls, and a tiny waxen hand. Hildegarde buried her face in her hands and sobbed; while Benny's gentle nurse smoothed her hair, and spoke softly and soothingly. This was what she had called a "frolic," — this! She had laughed, and come away as if to some gay party, and now a little child had died almost close beside her. Hildegarde had never been so near death before. The world seemed very dark to her, as she turned away, and followed Mrs. Murray into another room, where the convalescent children were at play. Here, as she took the remaining flowers from the box, little boys and girls came crowding about her, some on crutches, some with slings and bandages, some only pale and hollow-eyed; but all had a look of "getting well," and all were eager for the flowers. The easiest thing seemed to be to sit down on the floor; so down plumped Hildegarde, and down plumped the children beside her. Looking into the little pallid faces, her heart grew lighter, though even this was sad enough. But she smiled, and pelted the children with bouquets; and then followed much feeble laughter, and clutching, and tumbling about, while the good matron looked on well pleased.

"What's them?" asked one tiny boy, holding up his bunch.

"Those are pansies!" answered Hildegarde. "There are little faces in them, do you see? They smile when the sun shines, and when children are good."

"Nein," said a small voice from the outside of the circle, "dat iss Stiefmütterlein!"

"Du Blümlein fein!" cried Hildegarde. "Yes, to be sure. Come here, little German boy, and we will tell the others about the pretty German name."

A roly-poly lad of six, with flaxen hair and bright blue eyes, came forward shyly, and after some persuasion was induced to sit down in Hildegarde's lap. "See now!" she said to the others; " this pansy has a different name in Germany, where this boy — "

"Namens Fritzerl!" murmured the urchin, nestling closer to the wonderful Fräulein who knew German.

" Where Fritzerl came from. There they call it 'Stiefmütterlein,' which means ' little stepmother.' Shall I tell you why? See! In front here are three petals just alike, with the same colors and the same marking. These are the stepmother and her own two daughters; and here, behind, are the two step-daughters, standing in the background, but keeping close together like loving sisters. I hope the little stepmother is kind to them, don't you?"

" I 've got one!" piped up a little girl

with a crutch. "She's real good, she is. Only she washes my face 'most all day long, 'cause she's 'feared she won't do her duty by me. She brought me red jelly yesterday, and a noil-cloth bib, so's I wouldn't spill it on my dress. My dress's new!" she added, edging up to Hildegarde, and holding up a red merino skirt with orange spots.

"I see it is," said Hilda, admiringly; "and so bright and warm, isn't it?"

"I've got a grandma to home!" cried another shrill voice. "She makes splendid mittens! She makes cookies too."

"My Uncle Jim's got a wooden leg!" chimed in another. "He got it falling off a mast. He kin drive tacks with it, he kin. When I'm big I'm going to fall off a mast and git a wooden leg. You kin make lots o' noise with it."

"My grandma's got a wig!" said the

former speaker, in triumph. "I pulled it off one day. She was just like an aig on top. Are you like an aig on top?"

Here followed a gentle pull at one of Hildegarde's smooth braids, and she sprang up, feeling quite sure that her hair would stay on, but not caring to have it tumbling on her shoulders. "I think it is nearly time for me to go now," she was beginning, when she heard a tiny sob, and looking down, saw a very small creature looking up at her with round blue eyes full of tears. "Why, darling, what is the matter?" she asked, stooping, and lifting the baby in her strong young arms.

"I — wanted —" Here came another sob.

"What did you want? Come, we'll sit here by the window, and you shall tell me all about it."

"Ze uzzers told you sings, and — I — wanted — to tell you sings — too!"

"Well, pet!" said Hildegarde, drying the tears, and kissing the round velvet cheek, " tell me then!"

" Ain't got no — sings — to tell!" And another outburst threatened; but Hilda intervened hastily.

" Oh, yes, I am sure you have things to tell, lots of things; only you could n't think of them for a minute. What did you have for breakfast this morning?"

Baby looked doubtful. " Dat ain't a sing!"

" Yes, it is," said Hildegarde, boldly. " Come, now! I had a mutton chop. What did you have?"

" Beef tea," was the reply, with a brightening look of retrospective cheer, " and toasty strips!"

" *Oh*, how good!" cried Hilda. " I wish I had some. And what are you going to have for dinner?"

"Woast tsicken!" and here at last came a smile, which broadened into a laugh and ended in a chuckle, as Hilda performed a pantomime expressing rapture.

"I never heard of anything so good!" she cried. "And what are you going to eat it with, — two little sticks?"

"No–o!" cried Baby, with a disdainful laugh. "Wiz a worky, a weal worky."

"A walk!" said Hildegarde, puzzled.

"Es!" said Baby, proudly. "A atta worky, dess like people's!"

"Please, he means fork!" said a little girl, sidling up with a finger in her mouth. "Please, he's my brother, and we've both had tripod fever; and we're going home to-morrow."

"And the young lady must go home now" said Mrs. Murray, laying a kind hand on the little one's shoulder. "The man has come for you, Miss Grahame, and

I don't know how to thank you enough for all the pleasure you have given these dear children."

"Oh, no!" cried Hildegarde. "Please don't! It is I who must thank you and the children and all. I wish Rose — I wish my friend had come. She would have known; she would have said just the right thing to each one. Next time I shall bring her."

But "Nein! Müssen selbst kommen!" cried Fritzerl; and "You come, Lady!" shouted all the others. And as Hildegarde passed back through the long room where the sick children lay, Benny woke from his nap, and shouted, "Sing-girl! *my* sing-girl! come back soon!"

So, half laughing and half crying, Hildegarde passed out, her heart very full of painful pleasure.

CHAPTER X.

THE HOUSE IN THE WOOD.

ROSE was wonderfully better. Every day in the clear, bracing air of Bywood seemed to bring fresh vigor to her frame, fresh color to her cheeks. She began to take regular walks, instead of strolling a little way, leaning on her friend's stronger arm. Together the girls explored all the pleasant places of the neighborhood, which were many; hunted for rare ferns, with tin plant-boxes hanging from their belts, or stalked the lonely cardinal-flower, as it nodded over some woodland brook. Often they took the little boat, and made long expeditions down the pleasant river, — Hildegarde rowing, Rose couched at her ease in the stern. Once they came to the mouth of a stream which they pleased themselves by imagining to be unknown to mankind. Dipping the oars gently, Hildegarde drew the boat on and on, between high, dark banks of hemlock and pine and white birch. Here were cardinal-flowers, more than they had ever seen before, rank behind rank, all crowding down to the water's edge to see their beauty mirrored in the clear, dark stream. They were too beautiful to pick. But Hildegarde took just one, as a memento, and even for that one the spirit of the enchanted place seemed to be angered; for there was a flash of white barred wings, a loud shrill cry, and they caught the gleam of two fierce black eyes, as something whirred past them across the stream, and vanished in the woods beyond.

"Oh! what was it?" cried Hildegarde. "Have we done a dreadful thing?"

"Only a kingfisher!" said Rose, laughing. "But I don't believe we ought to have picked his flower. This is certainly a fairy place! Move on, or he may cast a spell over us, and we shall turn into two black stones."

One day, however, they had a stranger adventure than that of the Halcyon Stream, as they named the mysterious brook. They had been walking in the woods; and Rose, being tired, had stopped to rest, while Hildegarde pursued a "yellow swallow-tail" among the trees. Rose established herself on the trunk of a fallen tree, whose upturned roots made a most comfortable armchair, all tapestried with emerald moss. She looked about her with great content; counted the different kinds of moss growing within immediate reach, and found six; tried to decide which was the prettiest, and finding this impossible, gave it up, and fell to watching the play of the sunshine as it came twinkling through the branches of oak and pine. Green and gold!— those were the colors the fairy princes always wore, she thought. It was the most perfect combination in the world; and she hummed a verse of one of Hildegarde's ballads:—

"Gold and green, gold and green,
She was the lass that was born a queen.
Velvet sleeves to her grass-green gown,
And clinks o' gold in her hair so brown."

Presently the girl noticed that in one place the trees were thinner, and that the light came strongly through, as from an open space beyond. Did the wood end here, then? She rose, and parting the leaves, moved forward, till all of a sudden she stopped short, in amazement. For something strange was before her. In an open green space, with the forest all about it, stood a house,— not a deserted house, nor a tumble-down log-hut, such as one often sees in

Maine, but a trim, pretty cottage, painted dark red, with a vine-covered piazza, and a miniature lawn, smooth and green, sloping down to a fringe of willows, beyond which was heard the murmur of an unseen brook. The shutters were closed, and there was no sign of life about the place, yet all was in perfect order; all looked fresh and well cared for, as if the occupants had gone for a walk or drive, and might return at any moment. A drive? Hark! was not that the sound of wheels, even at this moment, on the neat gravel-path? Rose drew back instinctively, letting the branches close in front of her. Yet, she thought, there could be no harm in her peeping just for a moment, to see who these forest-dwellers might be. A fairy prince? a queenly maiden in gold and green? Laughing at her own thoughts, she leaned forward to peep through the leafy screen. What was her astonishment when round the corner came the familiar head of Dr. Abernethy, with the carryall behind him, Jeremiah driving, and Miss Wealthy sitting on the back seat! Rose could not believe her eyes at first, and thought she must be asleep on the tree-trunk, and dreaming it all. Her second thought was, why should not Miss Bond know the people of the house? They were her neighbors; she had come to make a friendly call. There was nothing strange about it. No! but it *was* strange to see the old lady, after mounting the steps slowly, draw a key from her pocket, deliberately open the door, and enter the house, closing the door after her. Jeremiah drove slowly round to the back of the house. In a few moments the shutters of the lower rooms were flung back. Miss Wealthy stood at the window for a few minutes, gazing out thoughtfully; then she disappeared.

Rose was beginning to feel very guilty, as

if she had seen what she ought not to see. A sense of sadness, of mystery, weighed heavily on her sensitive spirit. Very quietly she stole back to her tree-trunk, and was presently joined by Hildegarde, flushed and radiant, with the butterfly safe in her plant-box, a quick and merciful pinch having converted him into a "specimen" before he fairly knew that he was caught. Rose told her tale, and Hildegarde wondered, and in her turn went to look at the mysterious house.

"How *very* strange!" she said, returning. "I hardly know why it is so strange, for of course there might be all kinds of things to account for it. It may be the house of some one who has gone away and asked Cousin Wealthy to come and look at it occasionally. The people *may* be in it, and like to have the blinds all shut. And yet — yet, I don't believe it is so. I feel strange!"

" Come away!" said Rose, rising. " Come home ; it is a secret, and not our secret."

And home they went, very silent, and forgetting to look for maiden-hair, which they had come specially to seek.

But girls are girls; and Hildegarde and Rose could not keep their thoughts from dwelling on the house in the wood. After some consultation, they decided that there would be no harm in asking Martha about it. If she put them off, or seemed unwilling to speak, then they would try to forget what they had seen, and keep away from that part of the woods; if not —

So it happened that the next day, while Miss Wealthy was taking her after-dinner nap, the two girls presented themselves at the door of Martha's little sewing-room, where she sat with her sleeves rolled up, hemming pillow-cases. It was a sunny little room, with a pleasant smell of pennyroyal about it.

There was a little mahogany table that might have done duty as a looking-glass, and indeed did reflect the wonderful bouquet of wax flowers that adorned it; a hair-cloth rocking-chair, and a comfortable wooden one with a delightful creak, without which Martha would not have felt at home. On the walls were some bright prints, and a framed temperance pledge (Martha had never tasted anything stronger than shrub, and considered that rather a dangerous stimulant); and the Death-bed of Lincoln, with a wooden Washington diving out of stony clouds to receive the departing spirit.

"May we come in, Martha?" asked Hildegarde. "We have brought our work, and we want to ask you about something."

"Come in, and welcome!" responded Martha. "Glad to see you,— if you can make yourselves comfortable, that is. I'll get another chair from—"

"No, indeed, you will not!" said Hildegarde. "Rose shall sit in this rocking-chair, and I will take the window-seat, which is better than anything else ; so, there we are, all settled! Now, Martha—" She hesitated a moment, and Rose shrank back and made a little deprecatory movement with her hand ; but Hildegarde was not to be stopped. "Martha, we have seen the house in the wood. We just happened on it by chance, and we saw — we saw Cousin Wealthy go in. And we want to know if you can tell us about it, or if Cousin Wealthy would not like us to be told. You will know, of course."

She paused. A shadow had crossed Martha's cheerful, wise face ; and she sighed and stitched away in silence at her pillow-case for some minutes, while the girls waited with outward patience. At last, "I don't know why I should n't tell you, young ladies," she said slowly. "It's no harm, and no secret; only, of course, you would n't speak of it to her, poor dear!"

She was silent again, collecting her words; for she was slow of speech, this good Martha. "That house," she said at last, "belongs to Miss Bond. It was built just fifty years ago by the young man she was going to marry." Hildegarde drew in her breath quickly, with a low cry of surprise, but made no further interruption.

"He was a fine young gentleman, I 've been told by all as had seen him; tall and handsome, with a kind of foreign way with him, very taking. He was brought up in France, and almost as soon as he came out here (his people were from Castine, and had French blood) he met Miss Bond, and they fell in love with each other at sight, as they say. She lived here in this same house with her father (her mother was dead), and

she was as sweet as a June rose, and a picture
to look at. Ah! dear me, dear me! Poor
lamb! I never saw her then. I was a baby,
as you may say; leastwise a child of three
or four.

"Old Mary told me all about it when first
I came, — old Mary was housekeeper here
forty years, and died ten year ago. Well,
she used to say it was a picture to see Miss
Wealthy when she was expecting Mr. La Rose
(Victor La Rose was his name). She would
put on a white gown, with a bunch of pansies
in the front of it; they were his favorite
flowers, Mary said, and he used to call her
his Pansy, which means something in French,
I don't rightly know what; and then she
would come out on the lawn, and look and
look down river. Most times he came up in
his sail-boat, — he loved the water, and was
more at home on it than on land, as you may
say. And when she saw the white boat

coming round the bend, she would flush all up, old Mary said, like one of them damask roses in your belt, Miss Hilda; and her eyes would shine and sparkle, and she 'd clap her hands like a child, and run down to the wharf to meet him.   Standing there, with her lovely hair blowing about in the wind, she would look more like a spirit, Mary would say, than a mortal person.   Then when the boat touched the wharf, she would hold out her little hands to help him up; and he, so strong and tall, was glad to be helped, just to touch her hand.   And so they would come up to the house together, holding of hands, like two happy children.   And full of play they was, tossing flowers about and singing and laughing, all for the joy of being together, as you may say; and she always with a pansy for his button-hole the first thing; and he looking down so proud and loving while she fastened it in.   And most times he 'd bring her something, — a box of chocolate, or a new book, or whatever it was, — but old Mary thought she was best pleased when he came with nothing but himself. And both of them that loving and care-taking to the old gentleman, as one don't often see in young folks courting; making him sit with them on the piazza after tea, and the young man telling all he 'd seen and done since the last time; and then she would take her guitar and sing the sweetest, old Mary said, that ever was sung out of heaven. Then by and by old Mr. Bond would go away in to his book, and they would sit and talk, or walk in the moonlight, or perhaps go out on the water. She was a great hand for the water, Mary said; and never 's been on it since that time. Not that it 's to wonder at, to my mind. Ah, dear me!

"Well, my dears, they was to be married in the early fall, as it might be September.

He had built that pretty house, so as she need n't be far from her father, who was getting on in years, and she his only child. He furnished it beautiful, every room like a best parlor, — carpets and sofys and lace curt'ins, — there was nothing too good. But her own room was all pansies, — everything made to order, with that pattern and nothing else. It 's a sight to see to-day, fifty years since 't was all fresh and new.

"One day — my dear young ladies, the ways of the Lord are very strange by times, but we must truly think that they *are* his ways, and so better than ours, — one day Miss Wealthy was looking for her sweetheart at the usual time of his coming, about three o'clock in the afternoon. The morning had been fine, but the weather seemed to be coming up bad, Mary thought; and old Mr. Bond thought so, too, for he came out on the piazza where Mary was sorting out garden-herbs, and said, ' Daughter, I think Victor will drive to-day. There is a squall coming up ; it is n't a good day for the water.'

" And it was n't, Mary said ; for an ugly black cloud was coming over, and under it the sky looked green and angry.

" But Miss Wealthy only laughed, and shook her yellow curls back, — like curling sunbeams, Mary said they was, and said, ' Victor does n't mind squalls, Father dear. He has been in gales and hurricanes and cyclones, and do you think he will stop for a river flaw ? See ! there is the boat now, coming round the bend.'   And there, sure enough, came the white sailboat, flying along as if she was alive, old Mary said.   Miss Wealthy ran out on the lawn and waved her handkerchief, and they saw the young man stand up in the boat and wave his in return.   And then — oh, dear ! oh, dear me ! — Mary said, it seemed as if something black came rushing across the water and struck the boat like a hand; and down she went, and in a moment there was nothing to see, only the water all black and hissing, and the wind tearing the tree-tops."

"Oh! but he could swim!" cried Hildegarde, pale and breathless.

"He was a noble swimmer, my dear!" said Martha, sadly. "But it came too sudden, you see. He had turned to look at his sweetheart, poor young gentleman, and wave to her, and in that moment it came. He had n't time to clear himself, and was tangled in the ropes, and held down by the sail. Oh, don't ask me any more! But he was drowned, that is all of it. Death needs only a moment, and has that moment always ready. Eh, dear! My poor, sweet lady!"

There was a pause; for Rose was weeping, and Hildegarde could not speak, though her eyes were dry and shining.

Presently Martha continued: "The poor dear fell back into her father's arms, and he and Mary carried her into the house; and then came a long, sad time. For days and days they could n't make her believe but that he was saved, for she knew he was a fine swimmer; but at last, when all was over, and the body found and buried, they brought her a little box that they found in his pocket, all soaked with water, — oh, dear! — and in it was that pin, — the stone pansy, as she always wears, and will till the day she dies. Then she knew, and she lay back in her bed, and they thought she would never leave it. But folks don't often die that way, Miss Hilda and Miss Rose. Trouble is for us to live through, not to die by; and she got well, and comforted her father, and by and by she learned how to smile again, though that was not for a long time. The poor gentleman had made a will, giving the new house to her, and all he had; for he had no near kin living. Mr. Bond wanted her to sell it; but, oh! she would n't hear to it. All these years — fifty long years, Miss Hilda! — she has kept that house in apple-pie order. Once a month I go over, as old Mary did before me, and sweep it from top to bottom, and wash the windows. And three times a week she — Miss Bond — goes over herself, as you saw her to-day, and sits an hour or so, and puts fresh pansies in the vases; and Jeremiah keeps the lawn mowed, odd times, and everything in good shape. It's a strange fancy, to my idea; but there! it's her pleasure. In winter, when she can't go, of course, for the snow, she is always low-spirited, poor lady! I was *so* glad Mrs. Grahame asked her to go to New York last winter!

"And now, young ladies," said Martha, gathering up her pillow-cases, "I should be in my kitchen, seeing about supper.

That is all the story of the house in the wood. And you 'll not let it make you too sad, seeing 't was the Lord's doing; and to look at her now, you 'd never think but what her life had been of her own choosing, and she could n't have had any other."

Very quietly and sadly the girls went to their rooms, and sat hand in hand, and talked in whispers of what they had heard. The brightness of the day seemed gone; they could hardly bear the pain of sympathy, of tender pity, that filled their young hearts. They could not understand how there could ever be rallying from such a blow. They knew nothing of how long passing years turn bitter to sweet, and build a lovely " House of Rest " over what was once a black gulf of anguish and horror.

Miss Wealthy's cheerful face, when they went down to tea, struck them with a shock; they had almost expected to find it pale and tear-stained, and could hardly command their usual voices in speaking to her. The good lady was quite distressed. "My dear Rose," she said, "you look very pale and tired. I am quite sure you must have walked too far to-day. You would better go to bed very early, my dear, and Martha shall give you a hop pillow. Very soothing a hop pillow is, when one is tired. And, Hilda, you are not in your usual spirits. I trust you are not homesick, my child! You have not touched your favorite cream-cheese."

Both girls reassured her, feeling rather ashamed of themselves; and after tea Hildegarde read "Bleak House" aloud, and then they had a game of casino, and the evening passed off quite cheerfully.

CHAPTER XI.

"UP IN THE MORNING EARLY."

"ONE! two! three! four! five! six!" said the clock in the hall.

"Yes, I know it!" replied Hildegarde, sitting up in bed; and then she slipped quietly out and went to call Rose.

"Get up, you sleepy flower!" she said, shaking her friend gently, —

> "À l'heure où s'éveille la rose,
> Ne vas-tu pas te réveiller?"

Rose sighed, as she always did at the sound of the "impossible language," as she called the French, over which she struggled for an hour every day; but got up obediently, and made a hasty and fragmentary toilet, ending with a waterproof instead of a dress. Then each girl took a blue bundle and a brown bath towel, and softly they slipped downstairs, making no noise, and out into the morning air, and away down the path to the river. Every blade of grass was awake, and a-quiver with the dewdrop on its tip; the trees showered pearls and diamonds on the two girls, as they brushed past them; the birds were singing and fluttering and twittering on every branch, as if the whole world belonged to them, as indeed it did. On the river lay a mantle of soft white mist, curling at the edges, and lifting here and there; and into this mist the sun was striking gold arrows, turning the white to silver, and breaking through it to meet the blue flash of the water. Gradually the mist rose, and floated in the air; and now it was a maiden, a young Titaness, rising from her sleep, with trailing white robes, which caught on the trees and the points of rock, and hung in fleecy tatters on the hillside, and curled in snowy circles through the coves and hollows. At last she laid her long white arms over the hill-tops, and lifted her fair head, and so melted quite away and was gone, and the sun had it all his own way.

Then Hildegarde and Rose, who had been standing in silent delight and wonder, gave each a sigh of pleasure, and hugged each other a little, because it was so beautiful, and went into the boat-house. Thence they reappeared in a few minutes, clad in close-fitting raiment of blue flannel, their arms bare, their hair knotted in Gothic fashion on top of their heads. Then Hildegarde stood on the edge of the wharf, and rose on the tips of her toes, and joined her palms high above her head, then sprang into the air, describing an arc, and disappeared with a silver splash which rivalled that of her own sturgeon. But Rose, who could not dive, just sat down on the wharf and then rolled off it, in the most comfortable way possible. When they both came up, there was much puffing, and shaking of heads, and little gasps and shrieks of delight. The water by the wharf was nearly up to the girls' shoulders, and farther than this Rose could not go, as she could not swim; so a rope had been stretched from the end of the wharf to the shore, and on this she swung, like the mermaids on the Atlantic cable, in Tenniel's charming picture, and floated at full length, and played a thousand gambols. She could see the white pebbled bottom through the clear water, and her own feet as white as the pebbles (Rose had very pretty feet; and now that they were no longer useless appendages, she could not help liking to look at them, though she was rather ashamed of it). Now she swung herself near the shore, and caught hold of the twisted roots of the great willow that leaned over the water, and pulled the branches down till they fell like a green canopy over her; and now she splashed the water about, for pure pleasure of seeing the diamond showers as the sunlight caught them. But Hildegarde swam out into the middle of the river, cleaving the blue water with long, regular strokes; and then turned on her back, and lay contemplating the universe with infinite content.

"You are still in the shade, you poor Rosebud!" she cried. "See! I am right *in* the sparkle. I can gather gold with both hands. How many broad pieces will you have?" She sent a shower of drops toward the shore, which Rose returned with interest; and a battle-royal ensued, in which the foam flew left and right, and the smooth water was churned into a thousand eddies.

"I am the Plesiosaurus!" cried Hildegarde, giving a mighty splash. "Beware! beware! my flashing eyes, my floating hair!"

"Shade of Coleridge, forgive her!" exclaimed Rose, dashing a return volley of pearly spray. "And the Plesiosaurus had no hair; otherwise, I may say I have often observed the resemblance. Well, I am the Ichthyosaurus! You remember the picture in the 'Journey to the Centre of the Earth'?"

Hildegarde replied by plunging toward her, rearing her head in as serpentine a manner as she could command; and after a struggle the two mighty saurians went down together in a whirlpool of frothing waves. They came up quite out of breath, and sat laughing and panting on the willow root, which in one place curved out in such a way as to make a charming seat.

"Look at Grandfather Bullfrog!" said Rose. "He is shocked at our behavior. We are big enough to know better, are n't we, sir?" She addressed with deep respect an enormous brown bullfrog, who had come up to see what was the matter, and who sat on a stone surveying the pair with a look of indignant amazement.

"Coax! coax! Brek-ke-ke-kex!" cried Hildegarde. "That is the only sentence of frog-talk I know. It is in a story of Hans Andersen's. Do you see, Rose? He understands; he winked in a most expressive manner. Whom did you get for a wife, when you found Tommelise had run away from you; and what became of the white butterfly?"

The bullfrog evidently resented this inquiry into his most private affairs, and disappeared with an indignant " Glump!"

" Now you shall see me perform the great Nose and Toe Act!" said Hildegarde, jumping from the seat and swimming to the end of the wharf. " I promised to show it to you, you remember." She seized the great toe of her left foot with the right hand, and grasping her nose with the left, threw herself backward into the water.

Rose waited in breathless suspense for what seemed an interminable time; but at length there was a glimmer under the water, then a break, and up came the dauntless diver, gasping but triumphant, still grasping the nose and toe.

" I did n't — let go!" she panted. " I did n't — half — think I could do it, it is so long since I tried."

"I thought you would **never** come up again!" cried Rose. "It is a dreadful thing to do. You might as well be the Great Northern Diver at once. Are you sure there is n't a web growing between your toes?"

"Oh, that is nothing!" said Hildegarde, laughing. "You should see Papa turn back somersaults in the water. *That* is worth seeing! Look!" she added, a moment after, "there is a log floating down. I wonder if I can walk on it." She swam to the log, which was coming lazily along with the current; tried to climb on it, and rolled over with it promptly, to Rose's great delight. But, nothing daunted, she tried again and yet again, and finally succeeded in standing up on the log, holding out her arms to balance herself. A pretty picture she made, — lithe and slender as a reed, her fair face all aglow with life and merri-

"SHE FINALLY SUCCEEDED IN STANDING UP ON THE LOG."

ment, and the sunshine all round her. "See!" she cried, "I am Taglioni, the queen of the ballet. I had — a — *oh!* I *nearly* went over that time — I had a paper-doll once, named Taglioni. She was truly — lovely! You stood her on a piece of wood — just like this; only there was a crack which held her toes, and this has no crack. Now I will perform the Grand Pas de Fée! La-la-tra-la — if I cañ only get to this end, now! Rose, I forbid you to laugh. You shake the log with your empty mirth. La-la-la — " Here the log, which had its own views, turned quietly over, and the queen of the ballet disappeared with a loud splash, while Rose laughed till she nearly lost hold of her rope.

But now the water-frolic had lasted long enough, and it was nearly breakfast-time. Very reluctantly the girls left the cool delight of the water, and shaking themselves like two Newfoundland dogs, ran into the boat-house, with many exclamations over the good time they had had.

At breakfast they found Miss Wealthy looking a little troubled over a note which she had just received by mail. It was from Mrs. Murray, the matron of the Children's Hospital.

"Perhaps you would read it to me, Hilda dear!" she said. "I cannot make it out very well. Mrs. Murray's hand is very illegible, or it may be partly because I have not my reading-glasses." So Hilda read as follows: —

Dear Miss Bond, — Is there any one in your neighborhood who would take a child to board for a few weeks? Little Benny May, a boy of four years, very bright and attractive, is having a slow recovery from pneumonia, and has had one relapse. I dare not send him home, where he would be neglected by a very careless mother; nor can we keep him longer here. I thought you might possibly know of some good, motherly woman, who would take the little fellow-

and let him run about in the sunshine and drink milk, for that is what he needs.

With kind regards to your niece, whom I hope we shall see again,

Always sincerely yours,

ELIZABETH MURRAY.

Miss Wealthy listened attentively, and shook her head; buttered a muffin, stirred her tea a little, and shook her head again. "I can't think," she said slowly and meditatively, "of a soul. I really — " But here she was interrupted, though not by words. For Hildegarde and Rose had been exchanging a whole battery of nods and smiles and kindling glances; and now the former sprang from her seat, and came and knelt by Miss Wealthy's chair, and looked up in her face with mute but eloquent appeal.

"My dear!" said the old lady. "What is it? what do you want? Isn't the egg perfectly fresh? I will call—" But Hildegarde stayed her hand as it moved toward the bell.

"I want Benny!" she murmured, in low and persuasive tones, caressing the soft withered hand she had taken.

"A penny!" cried Miss Wealthy. "My *dear* child, certainly! Any small amount I will most gladly give you; though, dear Hilda, you are rather old, perhaps, — at least your mother might think so, — to — "

"Oh, Cousin Wealthy, how *can* you?" cried Hildegarde, springing up, and turning scarlet, though she could not help laughing. "I did n't say *penny*, I said *Benny!* I want the little boy! Rose and I both want him, to take care of. May n't we have him, *please?* We may not be motherly, but we are very sisterly, — at least Rose is, and I know I could learn, — and we would take such good care of him, and we *do* want him so!" She paused for breath; and Miss

Wealthy leaned back in her chair, and looked bewildered.

"A child! here!" she said; and she looked round the room, as if she rather expected the pictures to fall from the walls at the bare idea. In this survey she perceived that one picture hung slightly askew. She sighed, and made a motion to rise; but Hildegarde flew to straighten the refractory frame, and then returned to the charge.

"He is very small!" she said meekly. "He could sleep in my room, and we would wash and dress him and keep him quiet *all* the time."

"A child!" repeated Miss Wealthy, speaking as if half in a dream; "a little child, here!" Then she smiled a little, and then the tears filled her soft blue eyes, and she gave something like a sob. "I don't know what Martha would say!" she cried. "It might disturb Martha; otherwise—"

But Martha was at her elbow, and laid a quiet hand on her mistress's arm. "Sure we would all like it, Mam!" she said in her soothing, even tones. "'T would be like a sunbeam in the house, so it would. You'd better let the child come, Mam!"

So it was settled; and the very next day Hildegarde and Rose, escorted by Jeremiah, went to Fairtown, and returned in triumph, bringing little Benny with them.

Benny's eyes were naturally well opened, but by the time he reached the house they were staring very wide indeed. He held Hildegarde's hand very tight, and looked earnestly up at the vine-clad walls of the cottage. "Don't want to go in vere!" he said, hanging back, and putting his finger in his mouth. "Want to go back!"

"Oh, yes!" said Hildegarde. "You do want to come in here, Benny. That is what we have come for, you know. I am going to show you all sorts of pretty things, — picture-books, and shells, and a black kitty —"

But here she had touched a string that wakened a train of reflection in Benny's mind; his lip began to quiver. "Want — my — Nelephant!" he said piteously. "He's lef' alone — wiv fits. Want to go back to my Nelephant." An ominous sniff followed; an outbreak of tears was imminent.

Hildegarde caught him up in her arms and ran off toward the garden. She could *not* have him cry, she thought, just at the first moment. Cousin Wealthy would be upset, and might never get rid of the first impression. It would spoil everything! The little fellow was already sobbing on her shoulder, and as she ran she began hastily to repeat the first thing that came into her mind.

"Come, take up your hats, and away let us haste
    To the Butterfly's Ball and the Grasshopper's Feast.
    The trumpeter Gadfly has summoned the crew,
    And the revels are now only waiting for you !

"On the smooth-shaven grass by the side of the wood,
    Beneath a broad oak that for ages has stood,
    See the children of earth and the tenants of air
    For an evening's amusement together repair." .

The sobs had ceased, and Hildegarde paused for breath ; but the arm tightened round her neck, and the baby voice, still tearful, cried, " Sing !   Sing-girl want to sing ! "

" Oh me ! " cried Hildegarde, laughing. " You little Old Man of the Sea, how can I run and sing too ? "   She sat down under the laburnum-tree, and taking the two tiny hands in hers, began to pat them together, while she went on with the " Butterfly's Ball," singing it now to the tune of a certain hornpipe, which fitted it to perfection.   She had not heard the verses since she was a little girl, but she could never forget the delight of her childhood.

"And there came the Beetle, so blind and so black,
Who carried the Emmet, his friend, on his back.
And there came the Gnat, and the Dragon-fly too,
With all their relations, green, orange, and blue.

"And there came the Moth —"

At this moment came something else, more welcome than the moth would have been; for Rose appeared, bearing a mug in one hand, and in the other — what?

"Cow!" cried Benny, sitting upright, and stretching out both arms in rapture. "*My* cow! mine! all mine!"

"Yes, your cow, dear, for now!" said Rose, setting the treasure down on the table. "Look, Benny! she is such a good cow! She is going to give you some milk, — nice, fresh milk!"

The brown crockery cow was indeed a milk-jug; and Benny's blue eyes and Hildegarde's gray ones opened wide in amazement as Rose, grasping the creature's tail and tilting her forward, poured a stream of milk from her open mouth into the mug. The child laughed, and clapped his hands with delight.

"Where did you get it?" asked Hildegarde in a low tone, as she held the mug to Benny's lips.

"Saint Martha!" replied Rose, smiling. "It belonged to her grandmother. She brought it down just now, and said she had seen many a child quieted with it, and the little one would very likely be for crying at first, in a strange place! Is n't it nice?"

"Nice!" said Hildegarde; "I never want to drink out of anything else but a brown cow. Dear Martha! and observe the effect!"

Indeed, Benny was laughing, and patting the cow, and chattering to it, as if no such thing as a gray rubber elephant had ever existed. So fickle is childhood!

CHAPTER XII.

BENNY.

BENNY took possession of his kingdom, and ruled it with a firm, though for the most part an indulgent hand. Miss Wealthy succumbed from the first moment, when he advanced boldly toward her, and laying a chubby hand on her knee, said, "I like you. Is you' hair made of spoons? it is all silver."

Martha was his slave, and lay in wait for him at all hours with gingerbread-men and "cooky"-cows; while the two girls were nurses, playmates, and teachers by turns. Jeremiah wheeled him in the wheelbarrow, and suffered him to kick his shins, and might often be seen sedately at work hoeing or raking, with the child sitting astride on his shoulders, and drumming with sturdy heels against his breast. One member of the family alone resisted the sovereign charm of childhood; one alone held aloof in cold disdain, refusing to touch the little hand or answer the piping voice. That one was Samuel Johnson. The great Doctor was deeply offended at the introduction of this new element into the household. He had not been consulted; he would have nothing to do with it! So when Miss Wealthy introduced Benny to him the day after the child arrived, and waited anxiously for an expression of his opinion, the Doctor put up his great back, expanded his tail till it looked like a revolving street-sweeper, and uttering an angry "Fsss! spt!" walked away in high dudgeon.

Benny was delighted. "Funny old kyat!" he cried, clapping his hands. "Say 'Fsss' some more! Hi, ole kyat! I catch you."

Hildegarde caught him up in her arms as he was about to pursue the retiring dignitary, and Miss Wealthy looked deeply distressed.

"My dears, what shall we do?" she said. "This is very unfortunate. If I had thought the Doctor — but the little fellow is so sweet, I thought he would be pleased and amused. We must try to keep them away from each other. Or perhaps, if the little dear would try to propitiate the Doctor, — you have no idea how sensitive he is, and how he feels anything like disrespect, — if he were to *try* to propitiate him, he might — "

> "Vat ole kyat,
> He's too fat!"

shouted Benny, stamping his feet to emphasize the metre, —

> "Vat ole kyat
> He's too fat!
> *He* ought to go
> And catch a rat!"

"Come, Benny!" said Hildegarde, hastily, as she caught a glare from the Doctor's yellow eyes that fairly frightened her. "Come out with me and get some flowers." And as they went she heard Miss Wealthy's voice addressing the great cat in humble and deprecatory tones. As she walked about in the garden holding the child's hand, Hildegarde tried to explain to him that he must be very polite to Dr. Johnson, who was not at all a common cat, and should be treated with great respect.

But Benny's bump of reverence was small. "Huh!" he said. "*I* is n't 'fraid of kyats, sing-girl! You 's 'fraid, but I is n't. I had brown kitties, only I never seed 'em. Dr. Brown is a liar!" he added suddenly, with startling emphasis.

"Why, Benny!" cried Hildegarde. "What do you mean? You must n't say such things, dear child."

"He *is* a liar!" Benny maintained stoutly.

"He said ve brown kitties was in my froat. Vey was n't; so he's a liar. P'r'aps he's 'fraid too, but I is n't."

For several days the greatest care was taken to keep Benny out of Dr. Johnson's way. When the imperious mew was heard at the dining-room door after dinner, the child was hurried through with the last spoonfuls of his pudding, and whisked away to the parlor before the cat was let in. Nor would Miss Wealthy herself go into the parlor when the Doctor had finished his dessert, till she was sure that Benny had been taken out of doors. Hildegarde was inclined to remonstrate at this course of action, but Miss Wealthy would not listen to her.

"My dear," she said, "it does not do to trifle with a character like the Doctor's. I tremble to think what he might do if once thoroughly roused to anger. He is accustomed to respect, and demands it; and we must remember, my dear, that even in the domestic cat lies dormant the spirit of the Royal Bengal Tiger. No, my dear Hildegarde; we are responsible for this child's life, and we must at any cost keep him out of the Doctor's way."

But fate, which rules both cats and tigers, had ordained otherwise. One day Hildegarde had gone out to the stable to give a message to Jeremiah, and had left Benny playing by the back door, where Martha had promised to "have an eye to him" as she shelled the peas.

On her return, Hildegarde found that the child had run round to the front of the house; and she followed in that direction, led by the sound of his voice, which resounded loud and clear. Whom was he talking to? Hildegarde wondered. Rose was upstairs writing letters, and Cousin Wealthy was taking a nap. But now the words were plainly audible. " Dee ole kitty! Oh, *such* a dee ole kitty! Ole fat kyat, I lubby you."

Holding her breath, Hildegarde peeped round the corner of the house. There on the piazza, lay Dr. Johnson, fast asleep in the sunshine; and beside him stood Benny, regarding him with affectionate satisfaction. " I ain't seed you for yever so long, ole fat kyat!" he continued; "where has you been? You is *so* fat, you make a nice pillow for Benny. Benny go to sleep with ole fat kyat for a pillow." And to Hildegarde's mingled horror and amusement, the child curled himself up on the piazza floor, and deliberately laid his head on the broad black side of the sleeping lexicographer. The great cat opened his yellow eyes with a start, and turned his head to see " what thing upon his back had got." There was a moment of suspense. Hildegarde's first impulse was to rush forward and snatch the child away; her second was to stand perfectly still. " *Dee* ole kitty!" murmured Benny, in dulcet tones. "P'ease don't move! Benny *so* comfortable! Benny lubs his sweet ole pillow-kyat! Go to s'eep again, dee ole kitty!"

The Doctor lay motionless. His eyes wandered over the little figure, the small hands nestled in his own thick fur, the rosy face which smiled at him with dauntless assurance. Who shall say what thoughts passed in that moment through the mind of the representative of the Royal Bengal Tiger? Presently his muscles relaxed. His magnificent tail, which had again expanded to thrice its natural size, sank; he uttered a faint mew, and the next moment a sound fell on Hildegarde's ear, like the distant muttering of thunder, or the roll of the surf on a far-off sea-beach. Dr. Johnson was purring!

After this all was joy. The barriers were removed, and the child and the cat became inseparable companions. Miss Wealthy beamed with delight, and called upon the girls to observe how, in this most remarkable animal, intellect had triumphed over the feline nature. She was even a little jealous, when the Doctor forsook his hassock beside her chair to go and play at ball with Benny; but this was a passing feeling. All agreed, however, that a line must be drawn somewhere; and when Benny demanded to have his dinner on the floor with his " sweet ole kyat," four heads were shaken at him quite severely, and he was told that cats were good to play with, but not to eat with. In spite of which Rose was horrified, the next day, to find him crouched on all-fours, lapping from one side of the Doctor's saucer, while he, purring like a Sound steamer, lapped on the other.

Benny did another thing one day. Oh, Benny did another thing! Rose was teaching him his letters in the parlor, and he was putting them into metre, as he was apt to put everything, —

"*A*, B, *C*, D,
Fiddle, diddle,
Yes, I see!"

And with each emphasis he jumped up and down, as if to jolt the letters into his head.

"Try to stand still, Benny dear!" said gentle Rose.

But Benny said he could n't remember them if he stood still. "*A*, B, *C*, D! *E*, F, *jiggle* G!" This time he jumped backward, and flung his arms about to illustrate the "jiggle;" and — and he knocked over the peacock glass vase, and it fell on the marble hearth, and broke into fifty pieces. Oh! it was very dreadful. Mrs. Grahame had brought the peacock vase from Paris to Miss Wealthy, and it was among her most cherished trifles ; shaped like a peacock, with outspread tail, and shining with beautiful iridescent tints of green and blue. Now it lay in glittering fragments on the floor, and timid Rose felt as if she were too wicked to live, and wished she were back at the Farm, where there were no vases, but only honest blue willow-ware.

At this very moment the door opened, and Miss Wealthy came in. Rose shrank back for a moment behind the tall Japanese screen; not to conceal herself, but to gather her strength together for the ordeal. Her long years of illness had left her sensitive beyond description; and now, though she knew that she had done nothing, and that the child would meet only the gentlest of plaintive reproofs, her heart was beating so hard that she felt suffocated, her cheeks were crimson, her eyes suffused with tears. But Benny was equal to the emergency. His cheeks were very red, too, and his eyes opened very wide; but he went straight up to Miss Wealthy and said in a clear, high-pitched voice, —

"I've broke vat glass fing which was a peacock. I'm sorry I broke vat glass fing which was a peacock. I should n't fink you would leave glass fings round for little boys to hit wiv veir little hands and break vem. You is old enough to know better van vat. I know you is old enough, 'cause you' hair is all spoons, and people is old when veir hair is spoons, — I mean silver." Having said this with unfaltering voice, the child suddenly and without the slightest warning burst into a loud roar, and cried and screamed and sobbed as if his heart would break.

Rose was at his side in an instant, and told the story of the accident. And Miss Wealthy, after one pathetic glance at the fragments of her favorite ornament, fell to wiping the little fellow's eyes with her fine cambric handkerchief, and telling him that it was "no matter! no matter at all, dear!

Accidents *will* happen, I suppose!" she added, turning to Rose with a sad little smile. " But, my dear, pray get the dust-pan at once. The precious child might get a piece of glass into his foot, and die of lockjaw."

CHAPTER XIII.

A SURPRISE.

IT was a lovely August morning. Hildegarde and Rose had the peas to shell for dinner, and had established themselves under the great elm-tree, each with a yellow bowl and a blue-checked apron. Hildegarde was moreover armed with a book, for she had found out one can read and shell peas at the same time, and some of their pleasantest hours were passed in this way, the primary occupation ranging from pea-shelling to the paring of rosy apples or the stoning of raisins. So on this occasion the sharp crack of the pods and the soft thud of the

"Champions of England" against the bowl kept time with Hildegarde's voice, as she read from Lockhart's ever-delightful "Life of Scott." The girls were enjoying the book so much! For true lovers of the great Sir Walter, as they both were, what could be more interesting than to follow their hero through the varying phases of his noble life, — to learn how and where and under what circumstances each noble poem and splendid romance was written; and to feel through his own spoken or written words the beating of one of the greatest hearts the world ever knew.

Hildegarde paused to laugh, after reading the description of the first visit of the Ettrick Shepherd to the Scotts at Lasswade; when the good man, seeing Mrs. Scott, who was in delicate health, lying on a sofa, thought he could not do better than follow his hostess's example, and accordingly stretched himself at full length, plaid and all, on another couch.

"What an extraordinary man!" cried Rose, greatly amused. "How could he be so very uncouth, and yet write the 'Skylark'?"

"After all, he was a plain, rough shepherd!" replied Hildegarde. "And remember,

'The dewdrop that hangs from the rowan bough
Is fine as the proudest rose can show.'

Leyden was a shepherd, too, who wrote the 'Mermaid' that I read you the other day; and Burns was a farmer's boy. What wonderful people the Scots are!"

"On the whole," said Rose, after a pause, "perhaps it isn't so strange for a shepherd to be a poet. They sit all day out in the fields all alone with the sky and the sheep and the trees and flowers. One can imagine how the beauty and the stillness would sink into his heart, and turn into music and lovely words there. No one ever heard of a butcher-poet or a baker-poet — at least, I never did! — but a shepherd! There was the Shepherd Lord, too, that you told me about, and the Shepherd of Salisbury Plain, in a funny little old book that Father had; by Hannah More, I think it was. And was n't there a shepherd painter?"

"Of course! Giotto!" cried Hildegarde. "He was only ten years old when Cimabue found him drawing a sheep on a smooth stone."

"It was in one of my school-readers," said Rose. "Only the teacher called him Guy Otto, and I supposed it was a contraction of the two names, for convenience in printing. Then," she added, after a moment, "there was David, when he was 'ruddy, and of a beautiful countenance.'"

"And Apollo," cried Hildegarde, "when he kept the flocks of Admetus, you know."

"I don't know!" said Rose. "I thought Apollo was the god of the sun."

"So he was!" replied Hildegarde. "But Jupiter was once angry with him, and banished him from Olympus. His sun-chariot was sent round the sky as usual, but empty; and he, poor dear, without his golden rays, came down to earth, and hired himself as a shepherd to King Admetus of Thessaly. All the other shepherds were very wild and savage, but Apollo played to them on his lyre, and sang of all the beautiful things in the world, — of spring, and the young grass, and the birds, and — oh! everything lovely. So at last he made them gentle, like himself, and taught them to sing, and play on the flute, and to love their life and the beautiful world they lived in. And so the shepherds became the happiest people in the world, and the most skilful in playing and singing, and in shooting with bow and arrows, which the god also taught them; till at last the gods were jealous, and called Apollo back to Olympus. Isn't it a pretty story? I read it in 'Télémaque,' at school last winter."

"Lovely!" said Rose. "Yes, I think I should like to be a shepherd." And straightway she fell into a reverie, this foolish Rose, and fancied herself wrapped in a plaid, lying in a broad meadow, spread with heather as with a mantle, and here and there gray rocks, and sheep moving slowly about nibbling the heather.

And as Hildegarde watched her pure sweet face, and saw it soften into dreamy languor and then kindle again with some bright thought, another poem of the Ettrick Shepherd came to her mind, and she repeated the opening lines, half to herself: —

> "Bonny Kilmeny gaed up the glen;
> But it wasna to meet Duneira's men,
> Nor the rosy monk of the isle to see,
> For Kilmeny was pure as pure could be."

"Oh, go on, please!" murmured Rose, all unconscious that she was the Kilmeny of her friend's thoughts: —

> "It was only to hear the yorlin sing,
> And pu' the cress-flower round the spring;
> The scarlet hypp and the hindberrye,
> And the nut that hung frae the hazel-tree:
> For Kilmeny was pure as pure could be.
> But lang may her minny look o'er the wa',
> And lang may she seek i' the greenwood shaw;
> Lang the Laird of Duneira blame,
> And lang, lang greet or Kilmeny come hame.

> "When many a day had come and fled,
> When grief grew calm, and hope was dead;
> When mass for Kilmeny's soul had been sung,
> When the bedesman had prayed and the dead-bell
>   rung;
> Late, late in a gloamin', when all was still,
> When the fringe was red on the westlin hill,
> The wood was sear, the moon i' the wane,

The reek o' the cot hung over the plain,
Like a little wee cloud in the world its lane;
When the ingle lowed with an eiry leme,
Late, late in the gloamin' Kilmeny cam hame."

Here Hildegarde stopped suddenly; for some one had come along the road, and was standing still, leaning against the fence, and apparently listening. It was a boy about eleven years old. He was neatly dressed, but his clothes were covered with dust, and his broad-brimmed straw hat was slouched over his eyes so that it nearly hid his face, which was also turned away from the girls. But though he was apparently gazing earnestly in the opposite direction, still there was an air of consciousness about his whole figure, and Hildegarde was quite sure that he had been listening to her. She waited a few minutes; and then, as the boy showed no sign of moving on, she called out, "What is it, please? Do you want something?"

The boy made an awkward movement with his shoulders, and without turning round replied in an odd voice, half whine, half growl, "Got any cold victuals, lady?"

"Come in!" said Hildegarde, rising, though she was not attracted either by the voice, nor by the lad's shambling, uncivil manner, — "come in, and I will get you something to eat."

The boy still kept his back turned to her, but began sidling slowly toward the gate, with a clumsy, crab-like motion. "I'm a poor feller, lady!" he whined, in the same disagreeable tone. "I ain't had nothin' to eat for a week, and I've got the rheumatiz in my j'ints."

"*Nothing to eat for a week!*" exclaimed Hildegarde, severely. "My boy, you are not telling the truth. And who ever heard of rheumatism at your age? Do you think we ought to let him in, Rose?" she added, in a lower tone.

But the boy continued still sidling toward the gate. "I've got a wife and seven little children, lady! They're all down with the small-pox and the yeller — " But at this point his eloquence was interrupted, for Rose sprang from her seat, upsetting the basket of pods, and running forward, seized him by the shoulders.

"You scamp!" she cried, shaking him with tender violence. "You naughty monkey, how could you frighten us so? Oh, my dear, dear little lad, how do you do?" and whirling the boy round and tossing off his hat, she revealed to Hildegarde's astonished gaze the freckled, laughing face and merry blue eyes of Zerubbabel Chirk.

Bubble was highly delighted at the success of his ruse. He rubbed his hands and chuckled, then went down on all-fours and began picking up the pea-pods. "Sorry I made you upset the basket, Pink!" he said. "I say! how well you're looking! Isn't she, Miss Hilda? Oh! I didn't suppose you were as well as this."

He gazed with delighted eyes at his sister's face, on which the fresh pink and white told a pleasant tale of health and strength. She returned his look with one of such beaming love and joy that Hildegarde, in the midst of her own heartfelt pleasure, could not help feeling a momentary pang. "If my baby brother had only lived!" she thought. But the next moment she was shaking Bubble by both hands, and telling him how glad she was to see him.

"And now tell us!" cried both girls, pulling him down on the ground between them. "Tell us all about it! How did you get here? Where do you come from? When did you leave New York? What have you been doing? How is Dr. Flower?"

"Guess I 've got under Niag'ry Falls, by mistake!" said Bubble, dryly. "Let me see, now!" He rumpled up his short tow-colored hair with his favorite gesture, and meditated. - "I guess I 'll begin at the beginning!" he said. "Well!" (it was observable that Bubble no longer said "Wa-al!" and that his speech had improved greatly during the year spent in New York, though he occasionally dropped back into his former broad drawl.) "Well! it 's been hot in the city. I tell you, it 's been hot. Why, Miss Hilda, I never knew what heat was before."

"I know it must be dreadful, Bubble!" said Hildegarde. "I have never been in town in August, but I can imagine what it must be."

"I really don't know, Miss Hilda, whether

you can," returned Bubble, respectfully. " It isn't like any heat I ever felt at home.   Can you imagine your brains sizzling in your head, like a kettle boiling ? "

"Oh, don't, Bubble!" cried Rose. "Don't say such things ! "

" Well, it's true!" said the boy. " That's exactly the way it felt. It was like being in a furnace, — a white furnace in the day-time, and a black one at night; that was all the difference. I had my head shaved, — it's growed now, but I'm going to have it done again, soon as I get back, — and wore a flannel shirt and those linen pants you made, Pinkie. I tell you I was glad of 'em, if I did laugh at 'em at first — and so I got on. I wrote you that Dr. Flower had taken me to do errands for him during vacation ? " The girls nodded. " Well, I stayed at his house, — it's a jolly house ! — and 't was as cool there as anywhere. I went to the hospital with him every day, and I'm going to be a surgeon, and he says I can."

Hildegarde smiled approval, and Rose patted the flaxen head, and said, "Yes, I am sure you can, dear boy. Do you remember how you set the chicken's leg last year?"

"I told the doctor about that," said Bubble, "and he said I did it right. Was n't I proud! I held accidents for him two or three times this summer," he added proudly. "It never made me faint at all, though it does most people at first."

"Held accidents?" asked Hildegarde, innocently. "What do you mean, laddie?"

"People hurt in accidents!" replied the boy. "While he set the bones, you know. There were some very fine ones!" and he kindled with professional enthusiasm. "There was one man who had fallen from a staging sixty feet high, and was all—"

"Don't! don't!" cried both girls, in horror, putting their fingers in their ears.

"We don't want to hear about it, you dreadful boy!" said Hildegarde. "*We* are not going to be surgeons, be good enough to remember."

"Oh, it's all right!" said Bubble, laughing. "He got well, and is about on crutches now. Then there was a case of trepanning. Oh, that *was* so beautiful! You *must* let me tell you about that. You see, this man was a sailor, and he fell from the top-gallantmast, and struck —" But here Rose's hand was laid resolutely over his mouth, and he was told that if he could not refrain from surgical anecdotes, he would be sent back to New York forthwith.

"All right!" said the embryo surgeon, with a sigh; "only they're about all I have to tell that is really interesting. Well, it grew hotter and hotter. Dr. Flower did n't seem to mind the heat much; but Jock and I — well, we did."

"Oh, my dear little Jock!" cried Hildegarde, remorsefully. "To think of my never having asked for him. How is the dear doggie?"

"He's all right now," replied Bubble. "But there was one hot spell last month, that we thought would finish the pup. Hot? Well, I should — I mean, I should think it was! You had to put your boots down cellar every night, or else they'd be warped so you couldn't put 'em on in the morning."

"Bubble!" said Hildegarde, holding up a warning finger. But Bubble would not be repressed again.

"Oh, Miss Hilda, you don't know anything about it!" he said; "excuse me, but really you don't. The sidewalks were so hot, the bakers just put their dough out on them, and it was baked in a few minutes. All the

Fifth Avenue folks had fountain attachments
put on to their carriages, and sprinkled themselves with iced lavender water and odycolone
as they drove along; and the bronze statue
in Union Square melted and ran all over the
lot."

"Rose, what shall we do to this boy?"
cried Hildegarde, as the youthful Munchausen
paused for breath. "And you are n't telling
me a word about my precious Jock, you little
wretch!"

"One night," Bubble resumed,—"I'm in
earnest now, Miss Hilda,— one night it
seemed as if there was no air to breathe; as
if we was just taking red-hot dust into our
lungs. Poor little Jock seemed very sick;
he lay and moaned and moaned, like a baby,
and kept looking from the doctor to me, as
if he was asking us to help him. I was
pretty nigh beat out, too, and even the doctor
seemed fagged; but we could stand it better

than the poor little beast could. I sat and fanned him, but that did n't help him much, the air was so hot. Then the doctor sent me for some cracked ice, and we put it on his head and neck, and *that* took hold! 'The dog's in a fever!' says the doctor. 'We must watch him to-night, and if he pulls through, I'll see to him in the morning,' says he. Well, we spent that night taking turns, putting ice on that dog's head, and fanning him, and giving him water."

"My dear Bubble!" said Hildegarde, her eyes full of tears. "Dear good boy! and kindest doctor in the world! How shall I thank you both?"

"We were n't going to let him die," said Bubble, "after the way you saved his life last summer, Miss Hilda. Well, he did pull through, and so did we; but I was pretty shaky, and the morning came red-hot. The sun was like copper when it rose, and there seemed to be a sort of haze of heat, just pure heat, hanging over the city.   And Dr. Flower says, 'You're going to git out o' this!' says he."

"I don't believe he said anything of the kind!" interrupted Rose, who regarded Dr. Flower as a combination of Bayard, Sidney, and the Admirable Crichton.

"Well, it came to the same thing!" retorted Bubble, unabashed. "Anyhow, we took the first train after breakfast for Glenfield."

"Oh, oh, Bubble!" cried both girls, eagerly. "Not really?"

"Yes, really!" said Bubble. "I got to the Farm about ten o'clock, and went up and knocked at the front door, thinking I'd give Mrs. Hartley a surprise, same as I did you just now; but nobody came, so I went in, and found not a soul in the house. But I knowed — I *knew* she could n't be far off; for her knitting lay on the table, and the

beans — it was Saturday — were in the pot,
simmering away. So I sat down in the farmer's big chair, and looked about me. Oh,
I tell you, Miss Hilda, it seemed good!
There was the back door open, and the hens
picking round the big doorstep, just the way
they used, and the great willow tapping
against the window, and a pile of Summer
Sweetings on the shelf, all warm in the sunshine, you know, — only you weren't there,
and I kept kind o' hoping you would come
in. Do you remember, one day I wanted
one of them Sweetings, and you wouldn't
give me one till I'd told you about all the
famous apples I'd ever heard of?"

"No, you funny boy!" said Hildegarde,
laughing. "I have forgotten about it."

"Well, I hain't — haven't, I mean!" said
the boy. "I couldn't think of a single one,
'cept William Tell's apple, and Adam and
Eve, of course, and three that Lawyer

Clinch's red cow choked herself with trying to swallow 'em all at once, being greedy, like the man that owned her. So you gave me the apple, gave me two or three; and while I was eating 'em, you told me about the Hesperides ones, and the apple of discord, and that — that young woman who ran the race: what was her name? — some capital of a Southern State! Milledgeville, was it?"

"Atlanta!" cried Hildegarde, bursting into a peal of laughter; and "Atlanta! you goosey!" exclaimed Rose, pretending to box the boy's ears. "And it wasn't named for Atalanta at all, was it, Hildegarde?"

"No!" said the latter, still laughing heartily. "Bubble, it is delightful to hear your nonsense again. But go on, and tell us about the dear good friends."

"I'm coming to them in a minute," said Bubble; "but I must just tell you about

Jock first. You never saw a dog so pleased in all your life. He went sniffing and smelling about, and barking those little, short 'Wuffs!' as he does when he is tickled about anything. Then he went to look for his plate. But it was n't there, of course; so he ran out to see the hens, and pass the time o' day with them. They did n't mind him much; but all of a sudden a cat came out from the woodshed, — a strange cat, who did n't know Jock from a — from an elephant. Up went her back, and out went her tail, and she growled and spit like a good one. Of course Jock could n't stand that, so he gave a 'ki-hi!' and after her. They made time round that yard, now I tell you! The hens scuttled off, clucking as if all the foxes in the county had broke loose; and for a minute or two it seemed as if there was two or three dogs and half-a-dozen cats. Well, sir! — I mean, ma'am! at

last the cat made a bolt, and up the big
maple by the horse-trough. I thought she
was safe then; but Jock, he gave a spring
and caught hold of the eend of her tail,
and down they both come, kerwumpus, on
to the ground, and rolled eend over eend."
(It was observable that in the heat of nar-
ration Bubble dropped his school English,
and reverted to the vernacular of Glenfield.)
"But that was more than the old cat could
stand, and she turned and went for *him*.
Ha, ha! 't was 'ki, hi!' out of the other side
of his mouth then, I tell ye, Miss Hildy!
You never see a dog so scairt. And jest
then, as 't would happen, Mis' Hartley came
in from the barn with a basket of eggs, and
you may — you may talk Greek to me, if
that pup did n't bolt right into her, so hard
that she sat down suddent on the doorstep,
and the eggs rolled every which way. Then
I caught him; and the cat, she lit out some-

where, quicker 'n a wink, and Mis' Hartley sat up, and says she, ' Well, of all the world! Zerubbabel Chirk, you may just pick up them eggs, if you *did* drop from the moon!'"

CHAPTER XIV.

TELEMACHUS GOES A-FISHING.

AT this point Bubble's narrative was interrupted by the appearance of Martha, making demand for her peas. Bubble was duly presented to her; and she beamed on him through her spectacles, and was delighted to see him, and quite sure he must be very hungry.

"I never thought of that!" cried Hildegarde, remorsefully. "When did you have breakfast, and have you had anything to eat since?"

Bubble had had breakfast at half-past six, and had had nothing since. The girls were horrified.

"Come into the kitchen this minute!" said Martha, imperatively. So he did; and the next minute he was looking upon cold beef and johnny-cake and apple-pie, and a pile of doughnuts over which he could hardly see Martha's anxious face as she asked if he thought that would stay him till dinner. "For boys are boys!" she added, impressively, turning to Hildegarde; "and girls they are not, nor won't be."

When he had eaten all that even a hungry boy could possibly eat, Bubble was carried off to be introduced to Miss Wealthy. She, too, was delighted to see him, and made him more than welcome; and when he spoke of staying a day or two in the neighborhood, and asked if he could get a room nearer than the village, she was quite severe with him, forbade him to mention the subject again, and sent Martha to show him the little room in the ell, where she said he could be com-

fortable, and the longer he stayed the better.
It was the neatest, cosiest little room, just big
enough for a boy, the girls said with delight,
when they went to inspect it. The walls
were painted bright blue, which had rather
a peculiar effect; but Martha explained that
Jeremiah had half a pot of blue paint left
after painting the wheelbarrow and the pails,
and thought he might as well use it up.
Apparently the half pot gave out before
Jeremiah came to the chairs, for one of them
was yellow, while the other had red legs and
a white seat and back. But the whole effect
was very cheerful and pleasant, and Bubble
was enchanted.

The girls left him to wash his face and
hands, and brush the roadside dust from his
clothes. As he was plunging his face into the
cool, sparkling water in the blue china basin,
he heard a small but decided voice addressing
him; and looking up, became aware of a person

in kilts standing in the doorway and surveying him with manifest disapprobation.

"Hello, young un!" said Bubble, cheerily.
"How goes the world with you?"

"Vat basin ain't your basin!" responded
the person in kilts, with great severity.

Bubble looked from him to the basin, and
back again, with amused perplexity. "Oh!
it is n't, eh?" he said. "Well, that's a pity,
is n't it?"

"Vis room ain't your room!" continued
the new-comer, with increased sternness;
"vis bed ain't your bed! I 's ve boy of vis
house. Go out of ve back door! *Go* 'WAY!"

At the last word Benny stamped his foot,
and raised his voice to a roar which fairly
startled his hearer. Bubble regarded him
steadfastly for a moment, and then sat down
on the bed and began feeling in his pockets.
"I found something so funny to-day!" he
said. "I was walking along the road—"

"Go out of ye back door!" repeated Benny, in an appalling shout.

"And I came," continued Bubble, in easy, conversational tones, regardless of the vindictive glare of the blue eyes fixed upon him, — "I came to a great bed of blue clay. Not a bed like this, you know," — for Benny's glare was now intensified by the expression of scorn and incredulity, — "but just a lot of it in the road and up the side of the ditch. So I sat down on the bank to rest a little, and I made some marbles. See!" he drew from his pocket some very respectable marbles, and dropped them on the quilt, where they rolled about in an enticing manner. Benny was opening his mouth for another roar; but at sight of the marbles he shut it again, and put his hand in his kilt pocket instinctively. But there were no marbles in his pocket.

"Then," Bubble went on, taking apparently no notice of him, "I thought I would make some other things, because I did n't know but I might meet some boy who liked things." Benny edged a little nearer the bed, but spoke no word. "So I made a pear,"—he took the pear out and laid it on the bed,—"and a hen,"—the hen lay beside the pear,—"and a bee-hive, and a mouse; only the mouse's tail broke off." He laid the delightful things all side by side on the bed, and arranged the marbles round them in a circle. "And look here!" he added, looking up suddenly, as if a bright idea had struck him; "if you 'll let me stay here a bit, I 'll give you all these, and teach you to play ring-taw too! Come now!" His bright smile, combined with the treasures on the bed, was irresistible. Benny's mouth quivered; then the corners went up, up, and the next moment he was sitting on the bed, chuckling over the hen and the marbles, and the two had known each other for years.

"But look here!" said the person in kilts, breaking off suddenly in an animated description of the brown crockery cow, "you must carry me about on your back!"

"Why, of course!" responded Bubble. "What do you suppose I come here for?"

"And go on all-fours when I want you to!" persisted the small tyrant. "'Cause Jeremiah has a bone in his leg, and them girls" — oh, black ingratitude of childhood! — "won't. I don't need you for a pillow, 'cause I has my sweet old fat kyat for a pillow."

"Naturally!" said Bubble. "But if you should want a bolster any time, just let me know."

"Because I's ve boy of ve house, you see!" said Benny, in a tone of relief.

"You are that!" responded Bubble, with great heartiness.

By general consent, the second half of

Zerubbabel's narrative was reserved for the evening, when Miss Wealthy could hear and enjoy it. Hildegarde and Rose, of course, found out all about their kind friends at the Farm; and the former looked very grave when she heard that Mr. and Mrs. Hartley were expecting Rose without fail early in September, and were counting the days till her return. But she resolutely shook off all selfish thoughts, and entered heartily into the pleasure of doing the honors of the place for the new-comer.

Bubble was delighted with everything. It was the prettiest place he had ever seen. There never was such a garden; there never were such apple-trees, "except the Red Russet tree at the Farm!" he said. "*That* tree is hard to beat. 'Member it, Miss Hilda, — great big tree, down by the barn?"

"Indeed I do!" said Hilda. "Those are the best apples in the world, I think; and so beautiful, — all golden brown, with the bright scarlet patch on one cheek. Dear apples! I wish I might have some this fall."

Bubble smiled, knowing that Farmer Hartley was counting upon sending his best barrel of Russets to his favorite "Huldy;" but preserved a discreet silence, and they went on down to the boat-house.

When evening came, the group round the parlor-table was a very pleasant one to see. Miss Wealthy's chair was drawn up near the light, and she had her best cap on, and her evening knitting, which was something as soft and white and light as the steam of the tea-kettle. Near her sat Hildegarde, wearing a gown of soft white woollen stuff, which set off her clear, fresh beauty well. She was dressing a doll, which she meant to slip into the next box of flowers that went to the hospital, for a little girl who was just getting well enough to want "something to cuddle;" and her lap was full of rainbow fragments of silk and velvet, the result of Cousin Wealthy's search in one of her numerous piece-bags. On the other side of the table sat Rose, looking very like her name-flower in her pale-pink dress; while Bubble, on a stool beside her, rested his arm on his sister's knee, and looked the very embodiment of content. A tiny fire was crackling on the hearth, even though it was still August; for Miss Wealthy thought the evening mist from the river was dangerous, and dried her air as carefully as she did her linen. Dr. Johnson was curled on his hassock beside the fire; Benny was safe in bed.

"And now, Bubble," said Hildegarde, with a little sigh of satisfaction as she looked around and thought how cosey and pleasant it all was, "now you shall tell us about your fishing excursion."

"Well," said Bubble, nothing loath, "it was this way, you see. When I came back from the Farm, leaving Jock there, I found the doctor in his study, and the whole room full of rods and lines and reels, and all kinds of truck; and he was playing with the queerest things I ever saw in my life,— bits of feather and wool, and I don't know what not, with hooks in them. When he called me to come and look at his flies I was all up a tree, and did n't know what he was talking about; but he told me about 'em, and showed me, and then says he, ' I 'm going a-fishing, Bubble, and I 'm going to take you, if you want to go.' Well, I did n't leave much doubt in his mind about *that*. Fishing! Well, *you* know, Pinkie, there 's nothing like it, after all. So we started next morning, Doctor and I, and three other fel — I mean gentlemen. Two of 'em was doctors, and the third was a funny little man, not much bigger 'n me.

I wish 't you could ha' seen us start! Truck? Well, I should — say so! Rods, and baskets, and bait-boxes, and rugs, and pillows, and canned things, and camp-stools, and tents, and a cooking-stove, and a barrel of beer, and — "

" How much of this are you making up, young man ? " inquired Hildegarde, calmly; while Miss Wealthy paused in her knitting, and looked over her spectacles at Bubble in mild amazement.

" Not one word, Miss Hilda ! " replied the boy, earnestly. " Sure as you 're sitting there, we did start with all them — *those* things. Doctor, of course, knew 't was all nonsense, and he kept telling the others so; but they was bound to have 'em; and the little man, he would n't be separated from that beer-barrel, not for gold. However, it all turned out right. We were bound for Tapsco stream, you see; and when we came to the end of the railroad, we hired a sledge and a yoke of oxen, and started for the woods. Seven miles the folks there told us it was, but it took us two whole days to do it; and by the time we got to the stream, the city chaps, all 'cept Dr. Flower (and he really ain't half a city chap!) were pretty well tired out, I can tell you. Breaking through the bushes, stumbling over stumps and stones, and h'isting a loaded sledge over the worst places, was n't exactly what they had expected; for none of 'em but the doctor had been in the woods before. Well, we got to the stream; and there was the man who was going to be our guide and cook, and all that. He had two canoes, — a big one and a little one; he was going to paddle one, and one of us the other. Well, the little man — his name was Packard — said he 'd paddle the small canoe, and take the stove and the beer-barrel, ' 'cause they 'll need careful handling,' says he. The old guide looked at him, when he said that, pretty sharp, but he did n't say nothing ; and the rest of us got into the other canoe with the rest of the truck, after·we 'd put in his load. We started ahead, and Mr. Packard came after, paddling as proud as could be, with his barrel in the bow, and he and the stove in the stern. I wish 't you could ha' seen him, Miss Hilda! I tell you he was a sight, with his chin up in the air, and his mouth open. Presently we heard him say, ' This position becomes irksome ; I think I will change ' — but that was all he had time to say ; for before the guide could holler to him, he had moved, and over he went, boat and barrel and stove and all. Ha! ha! ha! Oh, *my !* if that was n't the most comical sight —"

" Oh, but, Bubble," cried Hildegarde, hastily, as a quick glance showed her that Miss Wealthy had turned pale, dropped her knitting, and put her hand up to the pansy brooch, "he was n't hurt, was he? Poor little man!"

"Hurt? not a mite!" responded Bubble. "He come up next minute, puffing and blowing like a two-ton grampus, and struck out for our canoe. We were all laughing so we could hardly stir to help him in; but the doctor hauled him over the side, and then we paddled over and righted his canoe. He was in a great state of mind! 'You ought to be indicted,' he says to the guide, 'for having such a canoe as that. It's infamous! it's atrocious! I — I — I — how dare you, sir, give me such a rickety eggshell and call it a boat?' Old Marks, the guide, looked at him again, and did n't say anything for a while, but just kept on paddling. At last he says, very slow, as he always speaks, 'I — guess — it's all right, Squire. This is a prohibition State, you know; and that's a prohibition boat, that's all.' Well, there was some talk about fishing the things up; but there was no way of doing it, and Dr. Flower said, anyhow, he did n't come to fish for barrels nor yet for cook-stoves; so we went on, and there they be — *are* yet, I suppose. Bimeby we came to Marks's camp, where we were to stay. It was a bark lean-to, big enough for us all, with a nice fire burning, and all comfortable. Doctor and I liked it first-rate; but the city chaps, — they said they must have their tents up, so we spent a good part of a day getting the things up."

" And were they more comfortable ? " asked Rose. " I suppose the gentlemen were not used to roughing it."

" Humph ! " responded Bubble, with sovereign contempt. " Mr. Packard set his afire, trying to build what he called a scientific fire, and came near burning himself up, and the rest of us, let alone the whole woods. And the second night it came on to rain, — my! how it did rain! and the second tent was wet through, and they were all mighty glad to come into the lean-to!"

"This seems to have been a severe experience, my lad," said Miss Wealthy, with gentle sympathy. "I trust that none of the party suffered in health from all this exposure."

"Oh, no, ma'am!" Bubble hastened to assure her. "It was splendid fun! splendid! I never had such a good time. I could fish for a year without stopping, I do believe."

Miss Wealthy's sympathetic look changed to one of mild disapproval, for she did not like what she called "violent sentiments." "So exaggerated a statement, my boy," she said gently, "is doubtless not meant to be taken literally. Fishing, or angling, to use a more elegant word, seems to be a sport which gives great pleasure to those who pursue it.

Dr. Johnson, it is true, spoke slightingly of it, and described a fishing-rod as a stick with a hook at one end, and — ahem! he was probably in jest, my dears — a fool at the other. But Izaak Walton was a meek and devout person; and my dear father was fond of angling, and — and — others I have known. Go on, my lad, with your lively description."

Poor Bubble was so abashed by this little dissertation that his liveliness seemed to have deserted him entirely for the moment. He hung his head, and looked so piteously at Hildegarde that she was obliged to take refuge in a fit of coughing, which made Miss Wealthy exclaim anxiously that she feared she had taken cold.

"Go on, Bubble!" said Hildegarde, as soon as she had recovered herself, nodding imperatively to him. "How many fish did you catch?"

"Oh, a great many!" replied the boy,

rather soberly. "Dr. Flower is a first-rate fisherman, and he caught a lot every day; and the other two doctors caught some. But Mr. Packard," — here his eyes began to twinkle again, and his voice took on its usual cheerful ring, — "poor Mr. Packard, he did have hard luck. The first time he threw a fly it caught in a tree, and got all tangled up, so 't he was an hour and more getting his line free. Then he thought 't would be better on the other side of the stream; so he started to cross over, and stepped into a deep hole, and down he sat with a splash, and one of his rubber boots came off, and he dropped his rod. Of all the unlucky people I ever saw! I tell you, 't was enough to make a frog laugh to see him fish! Then, of course, he 'd got the water all riled — "

" All — I beg your pardon ? — riled ? " asked Miss Wealthy, innocently.

"All muddy!" said Bubble, hastily; "so he could n't fish there no more for one while. And just then I happened to come along with a string of trout — ten of 'em, and perfect beauties! — that I'd caught with a string and a crooked pin; and that seemed to finish Mr. Packard entirely. Next day he had rheumatism in his joints, and stayed in camp all day, watching Marks making snow-shoes. The day after that he tried again, and fished all the morning, and caught one yellow perch and an eel. The eel danced right up in his face, — it did, sure as I 'm alive, Pink! — and scairt him so, I 'm blessed if he did n't sit down again — ho! ho! ho! — on a point o' rock, and slid off into the water, and lost his spectacles. Oh, dear! it don't seem as if it could be true; but it is, every word. The next day he went home. *He* 'll never go a-fishing again."

"Poor man! I should think not!" said

Rose, compassionately. "But is Dr. Flower — are all the others still there?"

"Gone home!" said Bubble. "We came out of the woods three days ago, and took the train yesterday. I never thought of such a thing as stopping; supposed I must go right back to work. But when the brakeman sung out, 'Next station Bywood!' Doctor just says quietly, 'Get your bag ready, Bubble! You're going to get out at this station.' And when I looked at him, all struck of a heap, as you may say, he says, 'Shut your mouth! you look really better with it shut. There is a patient of mine staying at this place, Miss Chirk by name. I want you to look her up, make inquiries into her case, and if you can get lodgings in the neighborhood, stay till she is ready to be escorted back to New York. It is all arranged, and I have a boy engaged to take your place for two weeks. Now, then! do

not leave umbrellas or packages in the train!
Good-by!' And there we were at the station; and he just shook hands, and dropped me off on the platform, and off they went again. Is n't he a good man? I tell you, if they was all like him, there would n't be no trouble in the world for anybody." And Rose thought so too!

CHAPTER XV.

THE GREAT SCHEME.

In the latter days of August came a hot wave. It started, we will say, from the Gulf, which was heated sevenfold on purpose, and which simmered and hissed like a gigantic caldron. It came rolling up over the country, scorching all it touched, spreading its fiery billows east and west. New York wilted and fell prostrate. Boston wiped the sweat from her intellectual brow, and panted in all the modern languages. Even Maine was not safe among her rocks and pine-trees; and a wavelet of pure caloric swept over quiet Bywood, and made its inhabitants very uncomfortable. Miss Wealthy could not remember any such heat. There had been a very hot season in 1853, — she remembered it because her father had given up frills to his shirts, as no amount of starch would keep them from hanging limp an hour after they were put on; but she really did not think it was so severe as this. She was obliged to put away her knitting, it made her hands so uncomfortable; and took to crocheting a tidy with linen thread, as the coolest work she could think of. Hildegarde and Rose put on the thin muslins which had lain all summer in their clothespress drawers, and did their best to keep Benny cool and quiet; read Dr. Kane's " Arctic Voyages," and discussed the possibility of Miss Wealthy's allowing them to shave Dr. Johnson.

Bubble spent much of his time in cracking ice and making lemonade, when he was not on or in the river.

As for Martha, she devoted herself to the concoction of cold dishes, and fed the whole family on jellied tongue, lobster-salad, ice-cream, and Charlotte Russe, till they rose up and blessed her.

When Flower-Day came, the girls braved the heat, and went to Fairtown with the flowers; Miss Wealthy reluctantly allowing them to go, because she was anxious, as they were, to know how the little patients bore the heat. They brought back a sad report. The sick children were suffering much; the hospital was like a furnace, in spite of all that could be done to keep it cool. Mrs. Murray sighed for a " country week " for them all, but knew no way of attaining the desired object, as most of the people interested in the hospital were out of town.

" Oh, if we could only find a place ! " cried Hildegarde, after she had told about the little pallid faces and the fever-heat in town. " If there were only some empty house," — she did not dare to look at Miss Wealthy as she said this, but kept her eyes on the river (they were all sitting on the piazza, waiting for the afternoon breeze, which seldom failed them), — "some quiet place, like Islip, where the poor little souls could come, for a week or two, till this dreadful heat is past." Then she told the story of Islip, with its lovely Seaside Home, where all summer long the poor children come and go, nursed and tended to refreshment by the black-clad Sisters. Miss Wealthy made no sign, but sat with clasped hands, her work lying idle in her lap. Rose was very pale, and trembled with a sense of coming trouble; but Hildegarde's cheeks were flushed, and her eyes shone with excitement.

There were a few moments of absolute silence, broken only by the hot shrilling of a locust in a tree hard by; then Zerubbabel

Chirk, calmly unconscious of any thrill in the air, any tension of the nerves, any crisis impending, paused in his whittling, and instead of carving a whistle for Benny, cut the Gordian knot.

"Why, there is a house, close by here," he said; "not more 'n half a mile off. I was going to ask you girls about it. A pretty red house, all spick and span, and not a soul in it, far as I could see. Why is n't it exactly the place you want?" He looked from one to the other with bright, inquiring eyes; but no one answered. "I 'm sure it is!" he continued, with increasing animation. "There 's a lawn where the children could play, and a nice clear brook for 'em to paddle and sail boats in, and gravel for 'em to dig in, — why, it was *made* for children!" cried the boy. "And as for the man that owns it, why, if he does n't want to stay there himself, why should n't he let some one else have it? —

unless he's an old hunks; and even if he is—" He stopped short, for Rose had seized his arm with a terrified grasp, and Hildegarde's clear eyes flashed a silent warning.

Miss Wealthy tottered to her feet, and the others rose instinctively also. She stood for a moment, her hand at her throat, her eyes fixed on Bubble, trembling as if he had struck her a heavy blow; then, as the frightened girls made a motion to advance, she waved them back with a gesture full of dignity, and turned and entered the house, making a low moan as she went.

"Send Martha to her, *quick!*" said Hildegarde, in an imperative whisper. "Fly, Bubble! the back door!"

Bubble flew, as if he had been shot from a gun, and returned, wide-eyed and open-mouthed, to find his sister in tears, and his adored Miss Hilda pacing up and down the piazza with hasty and agitated steps.

"What is it?" he cried in dismay. "What did I do? What is the matter with everybody? Why, I never—"

Hildegarde quieted him with a gesture, and then told him, briefly, the story of the house in the wood. Poor Bubble was quite overcome. He punched his head severely, and declared that he was the most stupid idiot that ever lived.

"I'd better go away!" he cried. "I can't see the old lady again. As kind as she's been to me, and then for me to call her a— I guess I'll be going, Miss Hilda; I'm no good here, and only doing harm."

"Be quiet, Bubble!" said Hildegarde, smiling in the midst of her distress. "You shall do nothing of the kind. And, Rose, you are not to shed another tear. Who knows? This may be the very best thing that could have happened. Of course I would n't have had you say it, Bubble, just in that way; but now that it *is* said, I — I think I am glad of it. I should not wonder — I really do hope that it may have been just the word that was wanted."

And so it proved. For an hour after, as the three still sat on the piazza, — two of them utterly disconsolate, the third trying to cheer them with the hope that she was feeling more and more strongly, — Martha appeared. There were traces of tears in her friendly gray eyes, but she looked kindly at the forlorn trio.

"Miss Bond is not feeling very well!" she said. "She is lying down, and thinks she will not come downstairs this evening. Here is a note for you, Miss Hilda, and a letter for the post."

Hildegarde tore open the little folded note, and read, in Miss Wealthy's pretty, regular hand, these words : —

My dear Hilda, — Please tell the boy that I do not mean to be an old hunks, and ask him to post this letter. We will make our arrangements to-morrow, as I am rather tired now.

Your affectionate cousin,

Wealthy Bond.

The letter was addressed to Mrs. Murray at the Children's Hospital; and at sight of it Hildegarde threw her arms round Martha's neck, and gave her a good hug. Her private desire was to cry; but tears were a luxury she rarely indulged in, so she laughed instead.

"Is it all right, Martha," she asked, — "really and truly right? Because if it is, I am the happiest girl in the world."

"It is all right, indeed, Miss Hilda!" replied Martha, heartily; "and the best thing that could have happened, to my mind. Dear gracious! so often as I 've wished for something to break up that place, so to speak, and make a living house 'stead of a dead one! And it never could ha' been done, in my thinking, any other way than this. So it's a good day's work you've done, and thankful she'll be to you for it when the shock of it is over." Then, seeing that the young people were still a little "trembly," as she called it, this best of Marthas added cheerfully: "It's like to be a very warm evening, I'm thinking. And as Miss Bond isn't coming down, wouldn't it be pleasant for you to go out in the boat, perhaps, Miss Hilda, and take your tea with you? There's a nice little mould of pressed chicken, do you see, and some lemon jelly on the ice; and I could make you up a nice basket, and 't would be right pleasant now, wouldn't it, young ladies?"

Whereupon Martha was called a saint and an angel and a brick, all in three breaths; and she went off, well pleased, to pack the basket, leaving great joy behind her.

Late that evening, when Hildegarde was going to bed, she saw the door of Miss Wealthy's room ajar, and heard her name called softly. She went in, and found the dear old lady sitting in her great white dimity armchair.

" Come here, my dear," said Miss Wealthy, gently. " I have something to show you, which I think you will like to see."

She had a miniature in her hand, — the portrait of a young and handsome man, with flashing dark eyes, and a noble, thoughtful face.

" It is my Victor ! " said the old lady, tenderly. " I am an old woman, but he is always my true love, young and beautiful. Look at it, my child ! It is the face of a good and true man."

" You do not mind my knowing ? " Hildegarde asked, kissing the soft, wrinkled hand.

" I am very glad of it," replied Miss

Wealthy, — " very glad! And in — in a little while — when I have had time to realize it — I shall no doubt be glad of this — this projected change. You see " — she paused, and seemed to seek for a word, — " you see, dear, it has always been Victor's house to me. I never — I should not have thought of making use of it, like another house. It is doubtless — much better. In fact, I am sure of it. It has come to me very strongly that Victor would like it, that it would please him extremely. And now I blame myself for never having thought of such a thing before. So, my dear," she added, bending forward to kiss Hildegarde's forehead, " besides the blessings of the sick children, you will win one from me, and — who knows? — perhaps one from a voice we cannot hear."

The girl was too much moved to speak, and they were silent for a while.

" And now," Miss Wealthy said very cheerfully, " it is bedtime for you, and for me too. But before you go, I want to give you a little trinket that I had when I was just your age. My grandmother gave it to me; and though I am not exactly your grandmother, I am the next thing to it. Open that little cupboard, if you please, and bring me a small red morocco box which you will find on the second shelf, in the right-hand corner. There is a brown pill-box next to it; do you find it, my love?"

Hildegarde brought the box, and on being told to open it, found a bracelet of black velvet, on which was sewed a garland of miniature flowers, white roses and forget-me-nots, wrought in exquisite enamel.

" I thought of it," said the old lady, as Hildegarde bent over the pretty trinket in wondering delight, " when I saw your forget-me-not room last winter. The clasp, you see, is a turquoise; I believe, rather a fine one.

"My grandfather brought it from Constantinople. A pretty thing; it will look well on
your arm. The Bonds all have good arms,
which is a privilege. Good-night, dear child!
Sleep well, and be ready to elaborate your
great scheme to-morrow."

CHAPTER XVI.

THE WIDOW BRETT.

So it came to pass that at the breakfast-table next morning no one was so bright and gay as Miss Wealthy. She was full of the new plan, and made one suggestion after another.

"The first thing," she said, "is to find a good housekeeper. There is nothing more important, especially where children are concerned. Now, I have thought of precisely the right person, — pre-cisely!" she added, sipping her tea with an air of great content. "Martha, your cousin Cynthia Brett is the very woman for the place."

" Truly, Mam, I think she is," said Martha, putting down the buttered toast on the exact centre of the little round mat where it belonged; " and I think she would do it too! "

" A widow," Miss Wealthy explained, turning to Hildegarde, her kind eyes beaming with interest, " fond of children, neat as *wax*, capable, a good cook, and makes butter equal to Martha's. My dears, Cynthia Brett was made for this emergency. Zerubbabel, my lad, are you desirous of attracting attention? We will gladly listen to any suggestion you have to make."

The unfortunate Bubble, who had been drumming on the table with his spoon, blushed furiously, muttered an incoherent apology, and wished he were small enough to dive into his bowl of porridge.

" And this brings me to another plan," continued the dear old lady. " Bixby, where

Cynthia Brett lives, is an extremely pretty little village, and I should like you all to see it. What do you say to driving over there, spending the night at Mrs. Brett's, and coming back the next day, after making the arrangements with her? Zerubbabel could borrow Mr. Rawson's pony, I am sure, and be your escort. Do you like the plan, Hilda, my dear?"

" Oh, Cousin Wealthy," cried Hildegarde, "it is too delightful! We should enjoy it above all things. But — no!" she added, "what would you do without the Doctor? You would lose your drive. Is there no other way of sending word to Mrs. Brett?"

But Miss Wealthy would not hear of any other way. It was a pity if she could not stay at home one day, she said. So when Mr. Brisket, the long butcher from Bixby, came that morning, and towering in the doorway, six feet and a half of blue jean, asked if they wanted "a-any ni-ice mut-ton toda-a-ay," he was intrusted with a note from Martha to her cousin, telling of the projected expedition, and warning her to expect the young ladies the next day but one.

The day came, — a day of absolute beauty, and though still very hot, not unbearable. Dr. Abernethy had had an excellent breakfast, with twice his usual quantity of oats, so that he actually frisked when he was brought round to the door. The whole family assembled to see the little party start. Miss Wealthy stood on the piazza, looking like an ancient Dresden shepherdess in her pink and white and silver beauty, and gave caution after caution: they must spare the horse up hill, and *never* trot down hill; "and let the good beast drink, dearie, when you come to the half-way trough, — not too much, but enough moderately to quench his thirst;" etc.

Martha beamed through her silver-rimmed spectacles, and hoped she'd given them enough lunch; while Benny, with his hand resting on the head of his " ole fat kyat," surveyed them with rather a serious air.

The girls had been troubled about Benny. They did not want to leave the little fellow, who had announced his firm intention of going with them; yet it was out of the question to take him. The evening before, however, Bubble had had a long talk with " ve boy of ve house; " and great was the relief of the ladies when that youthful potentate announced at breakfast his determination to stay at home and "take care of ve women-folks, 'cause Jim-Maria [the name by which he persistently called the melancholy prophet], he's gettin' old, an' somebody has to see to fings; and I's ve boy of ve house, so *I* ought to see to vem."

When the final moment came, however,

it seemed very dreadful to see his own Sing-girl drive away, and Posy, and the other boy too; and Benny's lip began to quiver, and his eyes to grow large and round, to make room for the tears. At this very moment, however, Jim-Maria, who had disappeared after bringing the horse to the door, came round the corner, bringing the most wonderful hobby-horse that ever was seen. It was painted bright yellow, for that was the color Jeremiah was painting the barn. Its eyes were large and black, which gave it a dashing and spirited appearance; and at sight of it the Boy of the House forgot everything else in heaven and earth. "Mine horse!" he cried, rushing upon it with outstretched arms, — "all mine, for to wide on! Jim-Maria, get out ov ve way! Goo-by, Sing-girl! goo-by, ev'ryboggy! Benny's goin' to ve Norf Pole!" and he cantered away, triumphant.

Then Hildegarde and Rose, seeing that all was well, made their adieus with a light heart, and Bubble waved his hat, and Miss Wealthy kissed her hand, and Martha shook her blue checked apron violently up and down, and off they went.

The little village of Bixby was in its usual condition of somnolent cheerfulness, that same afternoon. The mail had come in, being brought in Abner Colt's green wagon from the railway-station two miles away. The appearance of the green wagon, with its solitary brown bag, not generally too well filled, and its bundle of newspapers, was the signal for all the village-loungers to gather about the door of the post-office. The busy men would come later, when the mail was sorted; but this was the supreme hour of the loungers. They did not often get letters themselves, but it was very important that they should see who *did* get letters; and most of them had a newspaper to look for. Then the joy of leaning against the door-posts, and waiting to see if anything would happen! As a rule, nothing did happen, but there was no knowing what joyful day might bring a new sensation. Sometimes there was a dog-fight. Once — thrilling recollection! — Ozias Brisket's horse had run away ("Think 't 's likely a bumble-bee must ha' stung him; could n't nothin' else ha' stirred him out of a walk, haw! haw!") and had scattered the joints of meat all about the street.

To-day there seemed little chance of any awakening event beyond the arrival of the green cart. It was very warm; the patient post-supporters were nearly asleep. Their yellow dogs slumbered at their feet; the afternoon sun filled the little street with vivid golden light.

Suddenly the sound of wheels was heard, —

of unfamiliar wheels. The post-supporters
knew the creak or rattle or jingle of every
" team " in Bixby. There was a general stir,
a looking up the street, in the direction
whence the sound came; and then a gaping
of mouths, an opening of eyes, a craning of
long necks.

A phaeton, drawn by a comfortable-looking
gray horse, was coming slowly down the
street. It approached; it stopped at the
post-office door. In it sat two young girls:
one, tall, erect, with flashing gray eyes and
brilliant color, held the reins, and drew the
horse up with the air of a practised whip;
the other leaned back among the cushions,
with a very happy, contented look, though
she seemed rather tired. Both girls were
dressed alike in simple gowns of blue gingham; but the simplicity was of a kind unknown to Bixby, and the general effect was
very marvellous. The spectators had not yet

"'Can you tell us where Mrs. Brett lives?'"

shut their mouths, when a clattering of hoofs was heard, and a boy on a black pony came dashing along the street, and drew up beside the phaeton.

"No, it wasn't that house," he said, addressing the two girls. "At least, there was no one there. Say," he added, turning to the nearest lounger, a sandy person of uncertain age and appearance, "can you tell us where Mrs. Brett lives?"

"The Widder Brett?" returned the sandy person, cautiously. "Do ye mean the Widder Brett?"

"Yes, I suppose so," answered the boy. "Is there any other Mrs. Brett?"

"No, there ain't!" was the succinct reply.

"Well, where *does* she live?" cried the boy, impatiently.

"The Widder Brett lives down yender!" said the sandy person, nodding down the street. "Ye can't see the house from here, but go clear on to the eend, and ye 'll see it to yer right, — a yaller house, with green blinds, an' a yard in front. You 'kin to the Widder Brett?"

"No," said the tall young lady, speaking for the first time; "we are no relations. Thank you very much! Good-morning!" and with a word to the boy, she gathered up the reins, and drove slowly down the little street.

The post-supporters watched them till the last wheel of the phaeton disappeared round the turn; then they turned eagerly to one another.

"Who be they? What d' ye s'pose they want o' the Widder Brett?" was the eager cry. "Says they ain't no blood relation o' Mis' Brett's." "Some o' Brett's folks, likely!" "I allus heerd his folks was well off."

Meanwhile the phaeton was making its

way along slowly, as I said, for Rose was tired after the long drive.

"But not too tired!" she averred, in answer to Hildegarde's anxious inquiry. "Oh, no, dear! not a bit too tired, only just enough to make rest most delightful. What a funny little street!—something like the street in Glenfield, is n't it? Look! that might be Miss Bean's shop, before you took hold of it."

"Oh, worse, much worse!" cried Hildegarde, laughing. "These bonnets are positively mildewed. Rose, I see the mould on that bunch of berries."

"Mould!" cried Rose, in mock indignation. "It is bloom, Hilda,—a fine purple bloom! City people don't know the difference, perhaps."

"See!" said Hildegarde; "this must be 'the Widder Brett's' house. What a pretty little place, Rose! I am sure we shall like the good woman herself. Take the reins, dear, while I go and make sure. No, Bubble, I will go myself, thank you."

She sprang lightly out, and after patting Dr. Abernethy's head and bidding him stand still like the best of dears, she opened the white gate, which stuck a little, as if it were not opened every day. A tidy little wooden walk, with a border of pinks on either side, led up to the green door, in front of which was one broad stone doorstep. Beyond the pinks was a bed of pansies on the one hand; on the other, two apple-trees and a pleasant little green space; while under the cottage windows were tiger-lilies and tall white phlox and geraniums, and a great bush of southernwood; altogether, it was a front yard such as Miss Jewett would like.

Hildegarde lifted the bright brass knocker, — she was so glad it was a knocker, and not

an odious gong bell ; she *could* not have liked
a house with a gong bell,—and rapped gently.
The pause which followed was not strictly
necessary, for the Widow Brett had been
reconnoitring every movement of the new-
comers through a crack in the window-blind,
and was now standing in the little entry,
not two feet from the door. The good
woman counted twenty, which she thought
would occupy just about the time necessary
to come from the kitchen, and then opened
the door, with a proper expression of polite
surprise on her face.

" Good-day ! " she said, with a rising
inflection.

" How do you do ? " replied Hildegarde,
with a falling one. " Are you Mrs. Brett,
and are you expecting us ? "

" My name is Brett," replied the tall, spare
woman in the brown stuff gown ; " but I
was n't expectin' any one, as I know of.

Pleased to see ye, though! Step in, won't ye?"

"Oh!" cried Hildegarde, looking distressed. "Did n't you — have n't you had a letter from Martha? She promised to write, and said she was sure you would take us in for the night. I don't understand — "

"There!" cried Mrs. Brett. "Step right in now, do! and I'll tell you. This way, if *you* please!" and much flurried, she led the way into the best room, and drew up the hair-cloth rocking-chair, in which our heroine entombed herself. "I *do* declare," the widow went on, "I ought to be shook! There *was* a letter come last night; and my spectacles was broken, my dear, and I can't read Martha's small handwriting without 'em. I thought 't was just one of her letters, you know, telling how they was getting on, and I'd wait till one of the neighbors came in to read it to me. Well, there! and all the time she was telling me something, was she? and who might you be, dear, that was thinking of staying here?"

"I am Hilda Grahame!" said the girl, suppressing an inclination to cry, as the thought of Rose's tired face came over her. "If you will find the letter, Mrs. Brett, I will read it to you at once. It was to tell you that I was coming, with my friend, who is in the carriage now, and her young brother; and Martha thought there was no doubt about your taking us in. Perhaps there is some other house —"

"No, there is n't," said the Widow Brett, quickly and kindly, — "not another one. The idea! Of course I 'll take you in, child, and glad enough of the chance. And you Miss Hildy Grahame, too, that Marthy has told me so much about! Why, I 'm right glad to see ye, right glad!" She took Hildegarde's hand, and moved it up and down as if it were a pump-handle, her homely face shining with a cordiality which was evidently genuine. " Only," — and here her face clouded again, — " only if I 'd ha' known, I should have had everything ready, and have done some cleaning, and cooked up a few things. You 'll have to take me just as I am, I expect! However — "

" Oh, we *like* things just as they are! " cried Hildegarde, in delight. " You must not make any difference at all for us, Mrs. Brett! We shall not like it if you do. May I bring my friend in now ? "

" Well, I should say so! " cried the good woman. " She 's out in the carriage, you say ? I 'll go right out and fetch her in."

Rose was warmly welcomed, and brought into the house; while Hilda fastened Dr. Abernethy to the gate-post, and got the shawls and hand-bags out from under the seat.

"I expect you'd like to go right upstairs and lay off your things!" was Mrs. Brett's next remark. "I declare! I do wish 't I'd known! I swep' the spare chamber yesterday, but I hadn't any idea of its being used. Well, there! you'll have to take me as I am." She bustled upstairs before the girls, talking all the way. "I try to keep the house clean, but I don't often have comp'ny, and the dust doos gather so, this dry weather, and not keeping any help, you see — well, there! this is the best I've got, and maybe it'll do to sleep in."

She threw open, with mingled pride and nervousness, the door of a pleasant, sunny room, rather bare, but in exquisite order. The rag carpet was brilliant with scarlet, blue, and green; the furniture showed no smallest speck of dust; the bed looked like a snowdrift. Nevertheless, the good hostess went peering about, wiping the chairs with her apron, and repeating, " The dust *doos* gather so! I would n't set down, if I was you, till I 've got the chairs done off ! "

" Why, Mrs. Brett," cried Hildegarde, laughing merrily, " it is the chairs you should be anxious for, not ourselves. We are simply *covered* with dust, from head to foot. I think it must be an inch deep on my hat!" she continued, taking off her round " sailor" and looking at it with pretended alarm. " I don't dare to put it down in this clean room."

" Oh, *that* 's all right!" cried the widow, beaming. "Land sakes! I don't care how much dust you bring in, but I *should* be lawth to have you get any on you here. Well, there! now you need a proper good rest, I 'm sure, both of you. Would n't you like a cup o' tea now ? "

Both girls declined the tea, and declared that an hour's rest was all they needed ; so the good woman bade them "rest good!" and hurried downstairs, to fling herself into a Berserker fit of cooking. "Not a thing in the house!" she soliloquized, as she sifted flour and beat eggs with the energy of desperation, "except cookies and doughnuts; and Marthy always has everything so nice, let alone what they're used to at home. I'll make up a sheet of sponge-cake, I guess, first, and while it's baking I can whip up some chocolate frosting and mix a pan of biscuit. Le' me see! I might make a jelly-roll, while I'm about it, for there's some of Marthy's own currant jelly that she sent me last fall. They'd ought to have some hearty victuals for supper, I suppose; but I declare," — she paused, with the egg-beater in her hand, — "stuffed aigs'll have to do to-night, I guess!" she concluded with a sigh. "There isn't time to get a chicken ready. Well, there! If I'd ha' known! but they'll have to take me as I am. I might give 'em some fritters, though, to eat with maple surrup, just for a relish."

While these formidable preparations were going on against their peace of body, the two girls were enjoying an hour of perfect rest, each after her own manner. Rose was curled up on the bed, in a delicious doze which was fast deepening into sound sleep. Hildegarde sat in a low chair with a book in her hand, and looked out of the window. She could always rest better with a book, even if she did not read it; and the very touch of this little worn morocco volume — it was the "Golden Treasury" — was a pleasure to her. She looked out dreamily over the pleasant green fields and strips of woodland; for the house stood at the very end of the little village, and the country was before and around it. Under the window lay the back yard, with a white lilac-tree in blossom, and a well with a long sweep. Such a pleasant place it looked! A low stone-wall shut it in, the stones all covered with moss and gay red and yellow lichens. Beside the white lilac, there was a great elm and a yellow birch. In the latter was an oriole's nest; and presently Hildegarde heard the bird's clear golden note, and saw his bright wings flash by. "I like this place!" she said, settling herself comfortably in the flag-bottomed chair. She dropped her eyes to the book in her lap and read,—

> " Straight mine eye hath caught new pleasures
> While the landscape round it measures:
> Russet lawns, and fallows gray,
> Where the nibbling flocks do stray;
> Mountains, on whose barren breast
> The laboring clouds do often rest;
> Meadows trim with daisies pied,
> , Shallow brooks, and rivers wide."

Then her eyes strayed over the landscape again. " There must be a brook over there, behind that line of willows!" she thought. "I wonder if Milton loved willows. There are pines and monumental oaks in 'Il Penseroso,' but I don't remember any willows. It's a pity we have no skylarks here! I do want Rose to hear a skylark. Dear Rose! dear Milton! Oh — I am *so* comfortable!"

And Hildegarde was asleep.

CHAPTER XVII.

OLD MR. COLT.

SUPPER was over. The girls had laughingly resisted their hostess's appeal, " Just one more fritter, with another on each side to keep it warm, — though I don't 'know as they *are* fit to eat!" and on her positive refusal to let them help wash the dishes, had retired to the back doorstep, from which they could watch the sunset. Here they were joined by Bubble, who had found a lodging for himself, Dr. Abernethy, and the pony, in the family of Abner Colt, the mail-carrier. He took his place on the doorstep with the air of one who has fairly earned his repose.

"Well, Bubble," said Hildegarde, " tell us how you have fared."

"Oh, very well!" answered the boy, — "very well, Miss Hilda! They're a funny set over there at Mr. Colt's, but they seem very kind, and they have given me a nice little room in the stable-loft, so 't I can see to the Doctor any minute."

"How is the dear beast?" asked Rose. "I thought he went a little lame, after he got that stone in his foot."

"I have bathed the foot," said Bubble, "and it'll be all right to-morrow. Old Mr. Colt wanted to give me three different kinds of liniment to rub on it, but hot water is all it needs. He's a queer old fellow, old Mr. Colt!" he added meditatively. "Seems to live on medicine chiefly."

"What do you mean?" asked the girls.

"Why," said Bubble, "he came in to

supper — I had n't seen him before — with a big bottle under his arm, and a box of pills in his hand. He came shuffling in in his stocking-feet, and when he saw me he gave a kind of groan. 'Who's that?' says he. 'It's a boy come over from Bywood,' says Mrs. Abner, as they call her. 'He's goin' to stop here over night, Father. Ain't you glad to see him? — Father likes young folks real well!' she says to me. The old gentleman gave a groan, and sat down, nursing his big bottle as if it were a baby. 'D' ye ever have the dyspepsy?' he asked, looking at me. 'No, sir!' said I. 'Never had anything that I know of, 'cept the measles.' He groaned again, and poured something out of the bottle into a tumbler. 'You look kinder 'pindlin',' says he, shaking his head. 'I think likely you've got it on ye 'thout knowin' it. It's sub-tile, dyspepsy is, — dreadful sub-tile.'"

"What did he mean?—subtle?" asked Hilda, laughing.

"I suppose so!" replied the boy. "And then he took his medicine, groaning all the time and making the worst faces you ever saw. 'I reckon you'd better take a swallow o' this, my son!' he said. 'It's a pre-ventitative, as well's a cure.'"

"Bubble," cried his sister, "you are making this up. Confess, you monkey!"

"I'm not!" said Bubble, laughing. "It's true, every word of it. I *couldn't* make up old Mr. Colt! 'It's a pre-ventitative!' he says, and reaches out his hand for my tumbler. Then Abner, the young man, spoke up, and told him he guessed I'd be better without it, and that 't wasn't meant for young people, and so on. 'What is it, Mr. Colt?' I asked, seeing that he looked real — I mean very much — disappointed. He brightened up at once. 'It's Vino's Vegetable

Vivifier!' he said. 'It's the greatest thing out for dyspepsy. How many bottles have I took, Leory?' 'I believe this is the tenth, Father!' said Mrs. Abner. 'And *I* don't see as 't's done you a mite o' good!' she said to herself, but so 't I could hear. 'Thar!' says the old man, nodding at me, as proud as could be, 'd' ye hear that? Ten bottles I've took, at a dollar a bottle. Ah! it's great stuff. Ugh!' and he groaned and took a great piece of mince-pie on his plate. 'Oh, Father!' says the young woman, '*do* you think you ought to eat mince-pie, after as sick as you was yesterday?' He was just as mad as hops! 'Ef I'm to be grutched vittles,' he says, 'I guess it's time for me to be quittin'. I've eat mince-pie seventy year, man an' boy, and I guess I ain't goin' to leave off now. I kin go over to Joel's, if so be folks begrutches me my vittles here.' 'Oh, come, Father!' says Abner; 'you

know Leory did n't mean nothing like that.
Ef you 've got to have the pie, why, you 've
got to have it, that 's all.' The old man
groaned, and pegged away at the pie like
a good one. 'Ah!' he said, 'I sha'n't be
here long, anyway. Nobody need n't be afraid
o' *my* eatin' up their substance. Hand me
them doughnuts, Abner. Nothin' seems to
have any taste to it, somehow.'"

"Did he eat nothing but pie and doughnuts?" asked Hilda. "I should be afraid he
would die to-night."

"Oh," said Bubble, "you would n't believe me if I told you all the things he ate.
Pickles and hot biscuit and cheese — and
groaning all the time, and saying nobody
knowed what dyspepsy was till they 'd had
it. Then, when he 'd finished, he opened
the pill-box, which had been close beside his
plate all the time, and took three great fat
black pills. 'Have any trouble with yer liver?'

says he, turning to me again; ' there is nothin' like these pills for yer liver. You take two of these, and you'll feel 'em all over ye in an hour's time, — all over ye!' I thought 't was about time for me to go, so I said I must attend to the horse's foot, and went out to the stable. It was then that he brought me the three kinds of liniment, and wanted me to rub them all on, ' so's if one did n't take holt, another would.'"

" What a dreadful old ghoul!" cried Hildegarde, indignantly. " I don't think it's safe for you to stay there, Bubble. I know he will poison you in some way."

" You 're talking about Cephas Colt, I know," said the voice of Mrs. Brett; and the good woman appeared with her knitting, and joined the group on the doorstep. " He is a caution, Cephas is, — a caution! He's been dosing himself for the last thirty years, and it's a living miracle that he is alive to-day.

Abner and Leory have a sight o' trouble with him; but they 're real good and patient, more so 'n I should be. Did he show you his collection of bottles?" she added, turning to Bubble.

"No," replied the boy. "He did speak of showing me something; but I was in a hurry to get over here, so I told him I could n't wait."

"You 'll see 'em to-morrow, then!" said the widow. "It 's his delight to show 'em to strangers. Four thousand and odd bottles he has, — all physic bottles, that have held all the stuff he and his folks have taken for thirty years."

"Four — thousand — bottles!" cried her hearers, in dismay.

"And odd!" replied the widow, with emphasis. "He 's adding new ones all the time, and hopes to make it up to five thousand before he dies. Large ones and small, of course, and lotions and all. He takes every new thing that comes along, reg'lar. He has his wife's bottles all arranged in a shape, kind o' monument-like. They do say he wanted to set them up on her grave, but I guess that's only talk."

"How long ago did she die?" asked Rose.

"Three year ago, it is now!" said Mrs. Brett. "Dosed herself to death, we all thought. She was just like him! Folks used to say they had pills and catnip-tea for dinner the day they was married. You know how folks will talk! It's a fact though" — here she lowered her voice — "and I'd ought not to gossip about my neighbors, nor I don't among themselves much, but strangers seem different somehow, — anyhow, it *is* a fact that he wanted to put a scandalous inscription on her monument in the cemetery, and Abner wouldn't let him; the only time

Abner ever stood out against his father, as I know of."

" What was the inscription ? " asked Hildegarde, trying hard to look as grave as the subject required.

" Well, — you must n't say I told you ! " said the Widow Brett, lowering her voice still more, and looking about with an air of mystery, — " 't was

> ' Phosphoria helped her for a spell ;
> But Death spoke up, and all is well.'

'Sh ! you must n't laugh ! " she added, as the three young people broke into peals of laughter. " There ! I 'd ought not to have told. He did n't *mean* nothing improper, only to express resignation to the will o' Providence. Well, there ! the tongue 's an onruly member. And so you young ladies thought you 'd like to see Bixby, did ye ? "

she added, for the third or fourth time. "Well, I'm sure! Bixby'd oughter be proud. 'T *is* a sightly place, I've always thought. You must go over t' the cemetery to-morrow, and see what there is to see."

"Yes, we did want to see Bixby," answered straightforward Hildegarde; "but we came still more to see you, Mrs. Brett. Indeed, we have a very important message for you."

And beginning at the beginning, Hildegarde unfolded the great scheme. Mrs. Brett listened, wide-eyed, following the recital with appreciative motions of lips and hands. When it was over, she seemed for once at a loss for words.

"I — well, there!" she said; and she crumpled up her apron, and then smoothed it out again. "I — why, I don't know what *to* say. Well! I'm completely, as you may say, struck of a heap. I don't know what Marthy 's thinking of, I 'm sure. It is n't *me* you want, surely. You want a woman with faculty!"

" Of course we do!" cried both girls, laughing. " That is why we have come to you."

" Sho!" said Mrs. Brett, crumpling her apron again, and trying not to look pleased. "Why, young ladies, I could n't do it, no way in the world. There 's my chickens, you see, and my cow, let alone the house; not but what Joel (that 's my nephew) would be glad enough to take keer of 'em. And goin' so fur away, as you may say — though 't would be pleasant to be nigh Marthy — we was always friends, Marthy and me, since we was girls — and preserves to make, and fall cleanin' comin' on, and help so skurce as 't is — why, I don't know what Marthy 's think-in' of, really I don't. Children, too! why, I do love children, and I should n't never think I had things comfortable enough for 'em; not but that's a lovely place, pretty as ever I see. I helped Marthy clean it one spring, and such a fancy as I took to that kitchen, — why, there! and the little room over it; I remember of saying to Marthy, says I, a woman might live happy in those two rooms, let alone the back yard, with all that nice fine gravel for the chickens, I says. But there! I could n't do it, Miss Grahame, no way in the world. Why, I ain't got more 'n half-a-dozen aprons to my back; so now you see!"

This last seemed such a very funny reason to give, that the three young people could not help laughing heartily.

"Martha has dozens and dozens of aprons, Mrs. Brett," said Hildegarde. "She has a whole bureau full of them, because she is afraid her eyes may give out some day, and then she will not be able to make any more.

And now, just think a moment!" She laid
her hand on the good woman's arm, and
continued in her most persuasive tones:
" Think of living in that pleasant house,
with the pretty room for your own, and
the sunny kitchen, and the laundry, all
under your own management."

" " Set tubs!" said Mrs. Brett, in a pathetic
parenthesis. " If there's one thing I've
allers hankered after, more 'n another, it's a
set tub! "

" And the dear little children playing
about in the garden, and coming to you
with flowers, and looking to you as almost
a second mother —"

" Little Joel,"— cried the widow, putting
her apron to her eyes, and beginning to rock
gently to and fro, — " I've allus felt that
blessed child would ha' lived, if he'd ha'
been left with me. There! Joel's been a
good nephew, there could n't no one have

a better; but his wife and me, we never conjingled. She took the child away, and it peaked and pined from that day. Well, there! the ways are mysterious!"

"And you would take the chickens and the cow with you, of course," this artful girl went on; "for the children must have milk and eggs, and I never tasted more delicious milk than this of yours."

"I've no cause to be ashamed of the cow!" said the widow, still rocking. "There isn't a cow equal to her round Marthy's way. I've heerd Marthy say so. Sixteen quarts she gives, and I do 'clare it's most half cream. Jersey! there isn't many Jerseys round Marthy's way."

"And then the comfort you would be to Martha and to dear Miss Bond!" Rose put in. "Martha has a good deal of rheumatism in winter, you know, and she says you are such a good nurse. She told me how you rubbed her in her rheumatic fever. She thinks you saved her life, and I am sure you did."

" If I rubbed Marthy Ellen Banks one foot, I rubbed her a hundred miles!" said Mrs. Brett, with a faint gleam in her moist eyes. " 'From her tombstun back to a well woman is a good way,' Dr. Jones says to me, 'and that way you've rubbed Marthy Ellen, Mis' Brett!' says he. Good man Dr. Jones is, — none better! There is n't no one round Bixby can doctor my sciatica as he did when I was stayin' to Mis' Bond's last year. Mis' Bond, too, — well, there! she was a mother to me. Seemed like 't was more home there than Bixby was, since little Joel died. Mysterious the ways is! Mr. Rawlins well?" she added, after a moment's pause.

" Mr. — Oh, Jeremiah!" cried Hildegarde, after a moment of bewilderment.

"Jeremiah is very well, all except a cough; and, dear me! Mrs. Brett, I have n't given you his message. 'Tell Mrs. Brett,' he said, almost the last thing before we came away this morning, — 'tell Mrs. Brett she 'll *have* to come, to make me a treacle-posset for my cough. Not even Martha can make treacle-posset like hers!' Those were Jeremiah's very words, Mrs. Brett."

A faint color stole into the widow's thin cheeks. She sat up straight, and began to smooth out her apron. "Miss Grahame," she said emphatically, "I verily believe you could persuade a cat out of a bird's-nest. If it seems I 'm really needed over to Bywood — I don't hardly know how I *can* go — but — well, there! you 've come so fur, and I do like to 'commodate; so — well, I don't really see how I can — but — I will!"

CHAPTER XVIII.

JOYOUS GARD.

IT was the tenth day of September, and as pleasant a day as one could wish to see. The sun shone brightly everywhere; but Hildegarde thought that the laughing god sent his brightest golden rays down on the spot where she was standing. The House in the Wood no longer justified its name; for the trees had been cut away from around it, — only a few stately pines and ancient hemlocks remaining to mount guard over the cottage, and to make pleasant shady places on the wide, sunny lawns that stretched before and behind it. The brook no longer murmured unseen, but laughed now in the sunlight, and reflected every manner of pretty thing, — fleecy cloudlet, fluttering bird or butterfly, nodding fern or soldierly "cat-tail."

The house itself looked alert and wide-awake, with all its windows thrown open, and its door standing hospitably ajar, as if awaiting welcome guests. From an upper window came a sound of singing, for Rose was there, arranging flowers in the vases; from another direction was heard the ring of a hammer, as Bubble gave the last strokes to a wonderful cart which he had been making, and which was to be his contribution to the Country Home.

Hildegarde stood on the piazza, alone; her hands were full of flowers, and the "laughing light" of them was reflected in her bright, lovely face. She looked about her on the sunny greenery, on the blue shining stream, up to the bluer sky above. "This is the happiest day of my life!" said the girl, softly. She wondered what she had done, that all this joy and brightness should be hers. Every one was so good to her; every one had helped so kindly in the undertaking, from the beginning down to this happy end. There had been a good deal to be done, of course; but it seemed as if every hand had been outstretched to aid this work of her heart.

Cousin Wealthy, of course, had made it possible, and had been absorbed in it, heart and soul, as had all the others of the household. But there had also been so many pleasant tokens from outside. When Mrs. Brett arrived a week before, to take charge of the house, she brought a box of contributions from her neighbors in Bixby, to whom she had told the story of the Country Home, — scrap-books, comforters, rag-babies, preserves, pop-corn, pincushions, catsup, kettle-holders.   Bixby had done what it could, and the girls and Miss Wealthy and Martha were delighted with everything ; but there was much laughter when the widow pulled out a huge bottle of Vino's Vegetable Vivifier, and presented it, with a twinkle in her eye, as the gift of Mr. Cephas Colt. Nor had the scattered villagers of Bywood been less generous.   One good farmer had brought a load of wood ; another, some sacks of Early Rose potatoes ; a third presented a jar of June butter ; a fourth, some home-made maple-syrup.   The wives and daughters had equalled those of Bixby in their gifts of useful trifles ; and Rose, who was fond of details, calculated that there were two tidies for every chair in the house.

The boys of the neighborhood, who had at first shown a tendency to sit round on stumps and jeer at the proceedings, had now, at Hildegarde's suggestion, formed themselves into a Kindling-Wood Club, under Bubble's leadership; and they split wood every afternoon for an hour, with such good results that Jeremiah reckoned they would n't need no coal round this place; they could burn kindlin's as reckless as if they was somebody's else hired gal!

Then, the day before, a great cart had rumbled up to the door, bringing a packing-case, of a shape which made Hildegarde cry out, and clap her hands, and say, "Papa! I *know* it is Papa!" — which for the moment greatly disconcerted the teamster, who had no idea of carrying people's papas round in boxes. But when the case was opened, there was the prettiest upright piano that ever was seen; and sure enough, a note inside the cover said that this was "for Hildegarde's Hobby, from Hildegarde's Poppy." But more than that! the space between the piano and the box was completely filled with picture-books, — layers and layers of them; Walter Crane, and Caldecott, and Gordon Browne, and all the most delightful picture-books in the world. And in each book was written " The Rainy-Day Library; " which when Hildegarde saw, she began to cry, and said that her mother was the most blessed creature in the world.

But after all, the thing that had touched the girl's heart most deeply was the arrival, this very morning, of old Galusha Penny-packer, shuffling along with his stick, and bent almost double under the weight of a great sack which he carried on his back. Mrs. Brett had been looking out of the window, and announced that a crazy man was coming: " Looks like it, anyway. Had n't I better call Zee-rubble, Miss Grahame ? "

But Hildegarde looked out, recognized the old man, and flew to meet him. " Good-morning, Mr. Pennypacker ! " she cried cordially. "Do let me help you with that heavy bag! There! now sit down here in the shade, for I am sure you are very tired."

She brought a chair quickly; and the old man sank into it, for he was indeed exhausted by the long walk under his heavy burden. He gasped painfully for breath; and it was not till Hildegarde had brought him water, and fanned him diligently for some minutes, that he was able to speak.

"Thank ye!" he said at last, drawing out something that might once have been a handkerchief, and wiping his wrinkled face. "It's a warm day — for walkin'."

"Yes, indeed it is!" Hildegarde assented. "And it is a long walk from your house, Mr. Pennypacker. I fear it has been too much for you. Could you not have got one of the neighbors to give you a lift?"

"No! no!" replied the old man quickly,

with a cunning gleam in his sharp little eyes. "I'd ruther walk,—I'd ruther! Walkin' don't cost nothin'! They'd charged me, like's not, a quarter for fetchin' on me here. They think the old man's got money, but he hain't; no, he hain't got one red cent, — not for them he hain't." He paused, and began fumbling at the string of the sack. "Hearin' you was settin' up a horspittle here," he said, "I cal'lated to bring two or three apples. Children likes apples, don't they?" He looked up suddenly, with the same fierce gleam which had frightened Hildegarde and Rose so when they first saw him; but Hildegarde had no longer any fear of the singular old man.

"Yes, they do!" she said warmly. "I don't know of anything they like so well, Mr. Pennypacker. How very kind of you! And you came all this way on foot, to bring them?"

"The' warn't no shorter way!" replied old Galusha, dryly. "Thar'! I reckon them's good apples."

They were superb Red Astrakhans; every one, so far as Hildegarde could see, perfect in shape and beauty. Moreover, they had all been polished till they shone mirror-like. Hildegarde wondered what they had been rubbed with, but dismissed the thought, as one unwise to dwell upon.

"They's wuth money, them apples!" said the old man, after she had thanked him again and again for the timely gift. "Money!" he repeated, lingering on the word, as if it were pleasant to the taste. "Huh! there ain't nobody else on the yearth I'd ha' give so much as a core of one of 'em to, 'cept you, young woman."

"I'm sure you are extremely kind, Mr. Pennypacker!" was all Hildegarde could say.

"Ye've took thought for me!" said the old man. "The' ain't nobody took thought for old G'lushe Pennypacker, round here, not for a good while. Ye was to my place yesterday, warn't ye?" He looked up again, with a sudden glare.

"Yes," Hildegarde admitted, "I was; and my friend too. She knit the stockings for you, sir. I hope you liked them."

"Yes, yes!" said the old man, absently. "Good stockin's, good stockin's! Nice gal she is too. But—'t was you left the book, warn't it, hey?"

"Yes," said Hildegarde, blushing. "I am so fond of 'Robinson Crusoe' myself, I thought you might like it too."

"Hain't seen that book for fifty year!" said the old man. "Sot up all last night readin' it. It 'll be comp'ny to me all winter. And you—you took thought on me! —a young, fly-away, handsome gal, and old

G'lushe Pennypacker! Wal, 't won't be for-got here, nor yet yender!"

He gave an upward jerk of his head, and then passed his rag of a handkerchief over his face again, and said he must be going. But he did not go till he had had a glass of milk, and half-a-dozen of Mrs. Brett's doughnuts, to strengthen him for his homeward walk.

All this came back to Hildegarde, as she stood on the piazza; and as she recalled the softened, friendly look in the old man's eyes as he bade her good-by, she said again to herself, "This is the happiest day of my life!" The next day would not be so happy, for Rose and Bubble were going, — one to her home at Hartley's Glen, the other to his school in New York; and in a fortnight she must herself be turning her face homeward.

How short the summer had been! — had

there ever been such a flying season? — and yet she had done very little; she had only been happy, and enjoyed herself. Miss Wealthy, perhaps, could have told another story, — of kind deeds and words; of hours spent in reading aloud, in winding wools, in arranging flowers, in the thousand little helpfulnesses by which a girl can make herself beloved and necessary in a household. To the gentle, dreamy, delicate Rose, Hildegarde had really *been* the summer. Without this strong arm always round her, this strong sunny nature, helping, cheering, amusing, how could she have come out of the lifelong habits of invalidism, and learned to face the world standing on both feet? She could not have done it, Rose felt; and with this feeling, she probably would not have done it.

But, as I said, Hildegarde knew nothing of this. She had been happy, that was all.

And though she was going to her own beloved home, and to the parents who were
the greater part of the world to her, still
she would be sorry to leave this happiness
even for a completer one.

But hark! was that the sound of wheels?
Yes; they were coming.

"Cousin Wealthy!" cried the girl, running to the door. "Rose! Bubble! Martha! Mrs. Brett! Benny! Come out, all
of you! The stage is here!"

Out they came, all running, all out of
breath, save Miss Wealthy, who knew the
exact number of steps that would bring her
to the exact middle of the piazza, and
took these steps with her usual gentle pre-
cision of movement. She had no sooner
taken up the position which she felt to be
the proper one for her, than round the corner came the Bywood stage, — a long, lum-
bering, ramshackle vehicle, in which sat

Mrs. Murray, a kind-looking nurse, and the twelve convalescent children who were to have the first delights of the Country Home.

At sight of them Bubble began to wave his hat violently. "Hooray!" he shouted. "Three cheers for the young uns!"

"Hooray!" echoed Benny, flapping his hands about, as he had no hat to wave.

The children set up a feeble shout in reply, and waved heads, arms, and legs indiscriminately. Then ensued a scene of joyous confusion. The little ones were lifted out, kissed, and welcomed; their bundles followed;· and for a few minutes the quiet place was filled with a very Babel of voices.

High above them all rose the clarion tones of Benny, explaining to a former fellow-patient his present position in life. "I don't lives here!" he said; "I lives a little way off. I's ve boy of ve house where I lives, and I takes care of a whole lot of women-folks, and Jim Maria helps me, and vere's anover boy who does fings for me. It's bully, and I'm goin' to stay vere all my life long."

Mrs. Murray looked quickly at Miss Wealthy. "Does he know of his mother's death?" she asked in a low tone.

"No!" replied Miss Wealthy. "He has almost forgotten her, poor little lad! I fear she was not very kind to him. And I have decided to keep him, Mrs. Murray, and to give him a happy childhood, and then send him to a good school. He is a most lovable child, and it will be a privilege to have him, especially as my dear young relative is to leave me soon."

Both looked instinctively toward Hilde-garde, who was standing, flushed and radiant, the centre of a group of children, who clustered round her, pulling at her hands and clinging to her gown.

"What's the name of this place?" one little fellow was asking her. "I like this place! What is its name?"

"It is called Joyous Gard!" replied Hildegarde. "That was the name of a beautiful castle, long and long ago, which belonged to a very brave knight; and we think it will be a good name for your Country Home, because we mean to make it full of joy and happiness, and yet to guard you well in it. So Joyous Gard it is to be. Say it now, all of you, — 'Joyous Gard!'"

And "Joyous Gard!" shouted the children, their voices echoing merrily among the trees, and spreading away, till Rose, the romantic, wondered if some faint tone of it might not reach a pale shade called Lancelot du Lake, and bring him comfort where he sorrowed for his sins.

So in Joyous Gard let us leave our Hildegarde, — in each hand a child, around her many loving hearts, in her own heart great joy and light and love.   Let us leave her, and wish that all girls might know the cheer and happiness that was hers, not for that day only, but through all her days.

THE END.